D1827547

Feelin Some Type'a Way

Feat.

Aurora

Authored by: Success Bo

Highly Explicit W/Love

Highly Explicit W/Love

ACKNOWLEDGEMENTS

First, I would like to salute all the readers that

take the time out of their busy lives to read,

and especially read my novels. Also, I would

like to extend a salute to those that stuck with

me from the Streets to these Sheets of

paper…from my hood traditions to these

Urban Erotic Gangsta Fictions! And last but

never least, I salute and extend all of my love

to my children for waiting patient, and

continuing to Love Daddy until I got My Shit

Right!!!!

Love you all,

Unconditional!!!!

Chapter 1

It was Thursday June 19th, 2014, The Juneteenth Celebration in Denver, Colorado the Mile High City. The spirit of the city was at its peak, the entire atmosphere was vibrant. The weather was perfect…the Sun spreading it's magnificent warmth making the colors of colorful Colorado blend the beautiful sexiness and the griminess of gangstas into one. But as beautiful a day it was, the perfection of the day lasted momentary.

As a new model white on white Range Rover Sport sitting on 24s pulled into the traffic of City Park, the loud sound of automatic gunfire exploded loud and clear.

The driver of the Range Rover was a beautiful sista with golden honey skin. Her name was "Aurora". She was riding with another beautiful sista with smooth chocolate skin. Her name was "Poetry".

As the gunfire sounded they both dropped to the floor of the Range Rover, and as they ducked away from the gunfire Aurora panicky screamed out, "Bitch I told you these mutha-fuckas in Denver be trippin' waaayyy too much…we shoulda stayed our ass's in the "A"!"

As Poetry ducked low on the floor, she smiled and replied, "Bitch this aint nothin' new under the sun…niggas in the "A" be losin' their mutha-fuckan minds too…what you think niggas out that way is slippin' on they're Crippin'!"

Then the gunfire died down, but was replaced by the sound of screeching tires.

7

Everyone was revving up their powerful engines and making a clean and safe get away. Without any hesitation Aurora and Poetry was back in their seats, and as Aurora sped out keeping up with the traffic of the park she yelled, "Bitch I aint ever comin' back this way, ever again!"

Poetry smiled as she looked around at all the people, watching them run and hide for cover, but she replied with a little sarcasm, "Bitch you know you gon come back to the Eastside…where else yo-ass gon go…huh…Green Valley Ranch!"

Aurora let a little smile ease onto her expression as she followed the traffic out the park, and once they made it to the traffic of the streets Aurora asked, "Where are we headed?"

Poetry pulled out her iphone5 and read a message. After she read the message she glanced over to Aurora and said, "we mightiest well go by the 5 points and see what

Juneteenth is about down there, I mean since we're on this side of town."

Aurora nodded as she drove the Range Rover Sport. She made an illegal left turn on 26th and York St. An as she drove West on 26th Street headed to the 5 points she said, "Now bitch, I know you love this Eastside shit, but as soon as these mu-fuckas start Set Trippin' we up…and I mean 100 miles an hour back to the "A"!"

Poetry smiled as she bobbed her head to the sounds of Kendrick Lamar "Bitch don't kill my Vibe." Aurora pulled to a stop light on 26th and Downing St, and as they waited on the light to change green Poetry replied, "Bitch look at all these mutha-fuckas, I bet yo-ass anything that it's all the way crackin' on the points!"

Aurora looked at Poetry with a smirk on her expression and as the light change green she pulled off and said, "Bitch I know it's probably crackin' down here, but like I said, if I see any mutha-fuckin' Crip tryna get his Crip on-I'ma C-walk my ass back to my whip…and I put that on the game!"

Poetry smacked her tongue as she looked away from Aurora, but she said, "Bitch this is the Eastside!!!This is where Crips-Crip at…if yo diddy ass is scared go to church! Now find a parkin' space so I can get outta this mu-fucka…what's that sayin' the song says, 'Bitch Don't Kill My Vibe', na-mean!" They both looked each other over with a sassy but sexy expression until they cracked up laughing.

Then Aurora pulled into a parking space and after what seemed like an eternity, but was only 30 seconds, Poetry nodded and said, "Come on Bitch let's get out in traffic…we aint gon get no badder than what we already are."

Aurora shut the Range Rover off and within seconds they were walkin' on the 5 points-Welton Street.

Chapter 2

Aurora and Poetry walked down Welton Street until they made it in front of the Welton Street Café, Poetry seen some guys she knew from coming on the Eastside so much. One of the guys smiled at Poetry and replied, "Poetry in motion!"

Aurora glanced over the guy and his homies with the doodle face expression. Poetry smiled at them all and replied, "My nigga Rambo! What up wit' it?"

Poetry and Rambo shared a hug, then he smiled lightly and nodded his head and said, "You know what it is…the same thing every day: fast money, fast cars and fast ass Colorado CooChii!" Everyone laughed but Aurora.

As he said Colorado Coochii he let his eyes glaze over Aurora's from head to toe, and as he appraised her beauty, she stood in the perfect Mile High weather looking as flawless as she was.

Then Rambo turned back and looked at Poetry with a half smirk and a half smile as he asked, "Poetry, who is the Stranger?"

Aurora's anger quickly exploded at Rambo, she snapped, "Nigga I aint no mutha-fuckin stranger! Aint nuthin' strange about me, my name is Aurora!"

Rambo smiled at Poetry letting his gold teeth shine in the rays of the Sun. Then he looked back at Aurora with a serious expression etched across his face as he replied, "I know that's right ma', cause I'ma real nigga, I was taught that real niggas don't meet strangers!"

Then he stepped closer to Aurora with the grace of a playa. He extended his diamond flooded hand and wrist to her and introduced his self, he said, "Well since I now know that your name is Aurora, my name is Rambo, but you can call me Bo, (*then he smiled slyly and said*) and you can call me anytime."

Aurora smiled a light smile as she looked him over from head to toe quickly grading his style, but at the same time she let her mind run a plan of deceit, (*I wonder what this nigga is worth.*) She quickly rearranged her thoughts as she appraised him. He was Nautica down from head to feet.

Aurora replied, "A smooth nigga, huh!?!"

Rambo nodded again and as he shook hands with Aurora he responded, "I suppose."

Aurora smiled and as Rambo stepped back, Aurora looked him over again and subconsciously whispered, "I think I like his rhythm!"

As soon as Poetry heard Aurora whisper to herself, she smacked her tongue and revealed a little attitude as she grabbed Aurora's arm and her attention and walked off.

As they walked away from Rambo, Poetry whispered, "No bitch! You can't be feelin some type'a way about that nigga! He's waaayy too much for you, and besides that, he's a mutha-fuckin hoe…that's my nigga for the reals, but he aint worth a penny wit' a hole in it."

Aurora glanced back over her shoulder taking the time to really peep his style. She looked back with a serious expression. Rambo held his attention on her also, but he looked at her with a lustful expression. He held up his iphone5 in one hand and pointed at it with his other hand. Aurora nodded as to say yes.

Then as Rambo nodded in respond Poetry turned and looked over her shoulder at Rambo and stuck her tongue out at him. He frowned, until Poetry smiled innocently, and then he pointed towards Aurora, nodding and shrugging his shoulders. Poetry nodded and smiled as an agreement.

Then Aurora and Poetry blended into the crowd they walked slowly until they found themselves in front of the stage trapped in the sounds of "Interstate Ike" beating over every ones heads.

As they stood in front of the stage watching and listening to rappers perform,

Aurora asked Poetry, "Now bitch for the reals, what's up wit' yo-boy back there? He seems like he's cool people, but I aint got no time to waste tryna upgrade his ass."

Poetry heard Aurora, but ignored her as she acted like she was so into the performance of the rappers. Aurora bumped on Poetry's shoulder and yelled, "Bitch you hear me! What's up wit' yo-boy, Bo!"

Poetry laughed for a brief moment by herself, and then she said, "Bitch you done let Rambo dazzle yo-gullible ass, huh…he hit you wit' that quick ass game, now yo-little Coochii wet, huh!" Aurora smiled bashfully.

Then Poetry continued, "Well bitch you are my mu-fucka so I'ma keep it 100…that nigga is the shit for the reals! He's a real ass nigga out here, but he's a St. Louis nigga…and you aint gon upgrade that nigga, he's already upgraded outta control, and I mean like a mutha-fucka…yeah he is doin' the most, but all the good he's doin don't

change the fact that he's a mutha-fuckan dog!
For the reals Aurora, you shouldn't pay him
any attention. I mean he's really way too
much for you and your diddy ways, na-
mean."

Aurora looked back over her shoulder in
the direction where Rambo was, and as she
looked with deep concentration she thought to
herself, "*Aint no nigga too much for me.*"
Then she looked at Poetry and softly replied,
"I can handle that shit or any niggas shit…I
just aint got no time to be dealin' wit' no
gangsta shit."

Poetry looked back at Rambo for a
second then she said, "Naw he aint no gangsta
ass nigga like that, but his game is so gangsta
that you might can't handle that or let alone
the pack of Colorado Coochii that follows his
every move."

Aurora continued to stare back at
Rambo until her anger revved up, but she
said, "I'm ready and I can handle whoever or

whatever…the thing for the reals is, will he be able to handle me!"

Poetry looked at her with a surprised expression as she asked, "What was that you said, bitch?" Aurora was in a daze as she stared at Rambo until she shook her head snapping herself back into the reality of the moment, then she said, "can we leave…I'm ready to go!" Then she turned and started walking away from the stage.

Poetry shook her head smiling as she strolled along next to Aurora. As they stepped through the crowd and the streets of Juneteenth, they came back up on Rambo and his homies.

Rambo was so aware of them because of how he pays so much attention to detail, or should it be known, that he and Aurora both maintained eye contact every step she took.

Rambo let Aurora and Poetry step right in front of them, when he asked Aurora, "Hey ma', when you gon' let me *Cum* in Aurora to see you?"

Aurora tried to ignore him and his comment, but he stepped right to her. Poetry tried to interfere with the game by trying to step between them. But Rambo looked at her with a straight face as he said, "Come on Poetry that *hatin'* don't look good on you!" Poetry shrugged her shoulders, smiled and stepped aside.

Aurora shook her head as she looked Rambo in his face she said, "Un-un...get off my friend and I already heard about you...I aint no Colorado Coochii! So don't waste your time, cause for the reals, I really aint got that kinda time to waste, either!"

Rambo smacked his tongue as he stood in front of Aurora blocking her path. She looked him over from head to toe once again, and then Rambo said, "Come on ma', what you heard is make believe, that's all fiction *(he looked at Poetry as he spoke then back at Aurora)* get to know me, the real me...get the

19

true story!"

Aurora smacked her tongue as she looked around at all the onlookers that were paying too much attention to them. Then Rambo reached out and handed his iphone5 and said, "This is one of my lines, you hold it…I'll call you and give you the real me, and plus you don't have to give me your number, yet!"

Aurora mumbled, "Yet huh," she let her eyes glance over the iphone5 for a brief moment, and then she asked, "What if some'a you're other hoes or some Colorado Coochii calls?"

Rambo shook his head and replied, "Naw ma', I don't have no hoes in my life…but if anyone calls maybe your sexy voice will make them stop callin'."

Aurora smiled a little and replied, "Maybe huh!"

Then he looked at her from head to toe

again, and said, "Cause from the looks of things, I think I need you in my life."

Aurora took the iphone5 out of his hand, and as soon as she took the iphone5 he turned and walked back with his homies, but he said, "Answer every call until I call."

Aurora looked questionable at Poetry. Poetry shrugged her shoulders and said, "I told yo-ass he's somethin' else!" Aurora pushed the iphone5 into her Louis Vuitton bag, but as they walked back to the Range Rover she said, "I'ma give his ass one conversation, and if his ass can't blow, I'ma keep it pushin'!" Then they got in the Range Rover and rode out headed to the city of Aurora.

Chapter 3

Aurora and Poetry pulled up to the Aurora Mall, and as they walked towards the entrance of the mall a black on black 2012 S550 Mercedes Benz pulled along- side of them as they walked.

Aurora tried to look mean as she asked, "Who is this tryna ride all in our space?" Poetry looked and admired the whip, and then she said, "I don't know, but the whip is on hit, huh."

Then the window on the driver side slowly eased down. It was Rambo. As he smiled he looked right at Aurora and said, "I trust we me again, huh?"

Aurora looked at him with and annoyed expression as she asked, "Are you following me?"

Rambo continued to smile as he stopped the s550. He put the whip in park and stepped out and as he leaned against his whip he said, "Ma' I aint got know problem tryna following you, but I actually come to this mall every day."

Aurora smiled, and then tried to crack a joke, "Is this where you work on the low?" She laughed at her own joke for a short moment. Rambo's smile started to fade into a look of confidence as he replied, "Naw ma', on the low really aint my style. I'm probably job security for a lot of people that work around here."

Aurora smacked her tongue and said, "Yeah!"

Rambo nodded and replied, "Yeah!"

Then Aurora looked at Poetry and winked her eye slyly, then she looked back at Rambo and sassily said, "Well since you're here at the same time as us, I'm guessin', but are you gon pay for our fits, I mean you are Mr. Job Security…right!?!"

Rambo smiled at Aurora as he rubbed his hands together, and then said, "I normally don't pay for nuthin' but luxurious lace fronts, but this case I'll make an exception. But you better know I always get what I pay for, and I mean my money's worth."

Aurora smiled a little and then she softly replied, "We'll just have to see about that!"

Rambo smiled as he eased behind the steering wheel, but before he pulled off he said, "Look here ma', I'ma park my shit, but y'all can buy me an Orange Julius drink and meet me in the Macy's Men Store...that is if you really wanna see how far you think you can put your hands in life, na-mean."

Aurora nodded her head sexily and encouraging as she watched the s550 slowly pull off and away.

****

As Aurora and Poetry walked away from the Orange Julius restaurant Poetry cautiously said, "Bitch for the reals, you better slow your role, and not try and carry that nigga so fast, you know karma is a bitch! Especially when comes time for pay back...and you know pay back is a mutha!"

Aurora smacked her tongue as she walked, stepping as if she was Rippin' the

Runway, but she snapped back, "Bitch you the one that said that nigga was a hoe in the worse way, and that being true. It's only right for me to get in this nigga's style, and anyways, you know his ass is gon come at me wit' the best game he's got about this "na-na", and don't get me wrong." Poetry nodded and said, "Keep it 100!" Aurora continued, "I might submit to his game, but at least I can have the benefit of sayin' I got mine too, na-mean."

Poetry smiled a little and as they stepped in Macy's she said, "I'm just sayin' bitch, be careful of what you ask for…cause some'a these niggas out here is all bark no bite, but that nigga is most definitely all bark and all bite!"

Aurora smacked her tongue again, and as they stepped towards Rambo she whispered, "Don't give him more credit than he deserves, Floyd Mayweather is the only one that's undefeated." They both laughed quietly as they stepped to Rambo.

Aurora handed him his drink and looked at all the bags he already had, and said, "You shop kinda fast, huh."

Rambo nodded and replied, "I told you I come here every day, so I already know what I want when I wake up in the a.m." Then he snatched up his bags and said, "Come on let's do y'all, and I want y'all to remember what I really spend my bread on!"

Aurora bounced back on her leg real sassy and pursed her lips as she replied, "As long as you're spendin' your bread, you can dress me in whatever you like as long as you do it wit' class."

Rambo nodded, and then said, "Let's do it movin', and for your information, it really aint that important to me how you dress, as it is to how you undress."

Aurora looked at him with a look of surprise, and then as Rambo stepped leading the way he said, "Yeah I said that-meant that, and can't take it back, and the start of this shopping spree starts in Victoria's Secret and the finish line is my condo. Now if you're still tryna put your hand in my life, I'm headed this way, and if not you can let me get that iPhone back."

Aurora's pretty face balled into a frown as he walked off. Then she looked at Poetry and said, "He think he's the shit, huh! I know I'm gon hate his ass!" Poetry smiled as she was being entertained, but she whispered, "Your move, what you gon do?"

Aurora smacked her tongue and said, "Bitch what you think I'ma do, I'm headed to Victoria's Secret, I'ma put his shit to the test." Poetry smiled and said, "Bitch you already Colorado Coochii!" They high fived and laughed, and then they walked behind him headed on their shopping spree.

Chapter 4

Later on in the night, Aurora and Poetry pulled up to the Cold Crush Club and parked. Poetry looked at all the whips that lined the streets and said, "See bitch, this is how the Eastside be craccin'!"

As Aurora looked around and over all the whips she could feel her aggravation beginning to elevate. Poetry continued to revel in her excitement as she yelled, "Bitch, that whole line of whips is Bronco and Nugget players, and if them niggas is in there. it's really craccin'!"

Again Aurora looked around the area scanning the whips up and down the block unable to find what she was looking for. Poetry noticed something wrong with Aurora and asked, "What's wrong, bitch, let's go get our party on!" Aurora shook her head and replied, "I aint ready yet, you can go ahead, I'll catch you in there."

Poetry smacked her tongue angrily and said, "Naw bitch, un-un! That aint how this gon go...we been doin' this shit all day...naw this aint how it's gon go, for the reals!"

Aurora opened her Louis Vuitton Bag and pulled out the iPhone that Rambo left with her, and as she looked at it, Poetry yelled, "Aw-bitch that's what it is, you lookin' for Rambo!"

Aurora shoved the iPhone back into her bag and mumbled, "He still hasn't call for me yet."

Poetry shook her head and said, "Bitch you gotta slow your role…you got your legs open too wide for that nigga already and he aint did shit but sprinkle you wit' a few bread crumbs…don't let that dazzle you. Just play your game right and make him come after you, literally, and I bet you any kinda money that he really breaks bread wit' you, for real. I know that nigga, I know him, and once he sees how hot are you wit' all them professional niggas he gon go outta his way to take you away from them niggas…for the reals bitch, that's how niggas from the "E" are. Some niggas are professional in their own way, and you know them ball playin' niggas be tryna big bank hood niggas, but if it's one nigga that can stand up next to them rack for rack or status for status and still go hard it's Rambo. I aint bullshitting either, he's a real boss…now let's get our ass's in the club and that V.I.P. section so you can show all them bitches how to get chose by a boss!"

Aurora smiled as she listened to Poetry as she strengthened her confidence. Then she looked at herself in the mirror and said, "You right, huh. He just spent like a rack on me, so you know he gon chase his bread, huh."

Poetry nodded with a serious expression on her face as she replied, "I know you wanna walk in the club and on the scene wit 'a nigga, but bitch for the reals, it aint about the bitch that walks in wit' a nigga…as it is about the bitch that walks out wit' that nigga, na-mean." Aurora nodded and put her game face on. Then they both exited the Range Rover Sport and made their way to the club.

****

The club was doing exactly what Poetry said it would be doing. It was all the way live, people mingling, poppin bottles and just partying like rock stars, but not Aurora. She sat at the bar watching the entrance hoping and looking for Rambo. She could tell her patience was wearing thin, while her aggravation continued to build. She was unable to control her attitude, because the more and more niggas tried to talk to her the first thing they encountered was her attitude, because it was written across her face not her beauty.

Then the bartender sat a bottle of Cristal and a champagne glass in front of her. Aurora looked at the Cristal and then back at the bartender. The bartender nodded and said, "Compliments of the guy that bought the bar tonight in V.I.P...."

Then he pointed to one of the Nugget ball players. Aurora turned and looked at the guy in V.I.P., and just by how tall he was she knew he was a ball player.

The guy smile at Aurora, and nodded for her to come join him in the V.I.P. section, but she just smiled shyly, but did not commit. She turned back to the bar with a frown on her expression briefly because she finally noticed Rambo coming towards her.

As soon as Rambo stepped next to her she smiled and whined, as she said, "Dang Bo! I've been waitin' on you all night!" Rambo nodded and winked his eye, but she got up out of seat and shared a long awaited an intimate hug with him.

Then he stepped back and looked her over. She had on some coochii cutting shorts with a half shirt that revealed the clearest cut diamond on her belly ring. Her strongly and curvatious body stood on a pair of white Jimmy Choo Red Bottom stilettos.

Rambo nodded and then complimented her beauty, he said, "you look nice, ma'! Everything looks right on you."

Aurora smiled and replied, "Thanks to your taste and touch of class."

Rambo smiled and said, "You know it aint that hard to fix somethin' that aint broke, na-mean." She just nodded sexily as she moved the seat aside and pulled him next to her.

Rambo looked at the bottle of Cristal and said, "A bottle of Cristal, you doin big, huh?"

Aurora smiled, but she shook her head and said, "A guy from V.I.P. sent that bottle to me. He bought the bar tonight."

Rambo looked back to the V.I.P. section and seen the guy; mean muggin' with a smile. Rambo mumbled, "Nuggets, huh!" Then he grabbed the bottle and started pouring it out in the trash can until the bottle was all the way empty.

Aurora looked surprised as she asked, "What you do that for? I haven't even had any yet?"

Rambo shook his head a little, and then

waved the bar tender over to him and order another bottle of Cristal, then he said, "Ma', I don't need none of them niggas tryna sponsor you and never me…my money does a bomb ass job representing me…it's pretty obvious, look at you tonight, that's how my bread works!"

Aurora smiled as she reached to his chin and turned his face, she kissed a sexy and sweet kiss on his lips. Then she said, "That's right baby, be a Boss!"

As the bar tender sat the bottle of Cristal in front of them Rambo said, "Now let's toast to us and doin' somethin' wit' us!" But before he could pour any of the Cristal the Nugget player stepped up with the doodle face and attitude in his voice.

He said, "That bottle you poured out, I bought that for the beautiful young lady here."

Rambo shook his head as he looked serious and threating he said, "Naw-naw my nigg, that must'a been a mistake, cause she's wit' me…so you can charge that to the game, it's only a bottle of Cristal."

The Nugget player shrugged his shoulders and angrily replied, "I hear what you said, but I need my bread back for that bottle you touched!"

Rambo's anger quickly revved up. He shoved the nigga away from him and yelled, "Nigga-Please!"

Just as the Nugget player regained his balance the entire club looked as if it rushed to that section. Most of the niggas rushed outta the V.I.P. section, but outta nowhere, most of the street niggas rushed over to Rambo's defense.

The bouncer's stepped in between everyone before the club turned into a big bar fight. Rambo looked at the nigga with a mean mug expression until he regained his composure, and then he grabbed his bottle of Cristal and with his other hand he interlocked fingers with Aurora and stepped towards the exit.

Before they disappeared walking out the door Aurora heard her name being called. She knew it could only be Poetry. Aurora turned and tossed Poetry the key to the Range Rover and said, "I'll call you tomorrow!"

Poetry caught the key out of the air and smiled as she watched them walk to Rambo's whip. Poetry stood in the doorway watching them smiling until she seen them ride off and out.

Chapter 5

As Rambo drove the s550 Mercedes Benz Aurora reclined back in the passenger seat letting the smooth sounds of "Sevyn Streeter-It Won't Stop" set the rhythm of her heart, body and the mood.

Rambo held the bottle of Cristal between his legs as he drove. Aurora let her eyes set on the downtown skyline as she rode and hormonally said, "Babe, I really never knew how pretty downtown was."

Rambo just nodded as he continued to enjoy the smooth comforts of the s550 as they glided across the streets of downtown Denver Colorado. Aurora asked in a very seducing voice, "Are we headed to your condo?"

He nodded as he peeped at her and said, "Yeah my crib is the most peaceful place in the world to me, you'll be the first female I've ever had in my palace."

Aurora smiled an enticing smile and then leaned over and grabbed the bottle of Cristal from between Rambo's leg's, and after she raised the bottle to her lips and took a swig she asked, "Why me, I mean, what makes me so special, and why are you comfortable enough to take me there?"

He looked at her as she took another sip of the Cristal, but he replied, "I knew from first sight that it was somethin' special about you, and I wanna know what that is, ma'."

Aurora leaned over and kissed him on his cheek and then started sucking on his neck very sexily as he drove, and at the same time she let her free hand ease down into his lap. She started to caress his quickly growing hard dick as she let her warm breath and the tip of her tongue trace moist circles on his neck.

Rambo spoke low and slow as he let Aurora's sexy charms work on him saying, "Yeah ma' it's like I said, I'ma real ass nigga and real recognizes real, and I know it's somethin' really real about you because I'm normally not this magnetized by nuthin', anyone, or anything…but money."

Aurora hummed and agreed as she kissed down his chest. She unbuttoned his True Religion jeans and unleashed his long thick rock hard chocolate dick. But in-between kisses she said, "That's cause I aint just any average anyone…I'm Aurora, the goddess!"

Then she lowered her head and with her

face and hot breath inches away from his dickhead she let the tip of her tongue ease across the head of his dick, tasting the sweet cream that oozed from him, and as her taste buds tingled she moaned and whispered, "I'ma love givin' you wet kisses...I hope your Condo is a long way from here."

Rambo let out a strong sigh as Aurora swallowed in as much dick that her mouth would allow. Rambo inhaled a deep breath and whispered, "mmm huh ma', that's it...handle me properly!"

Aurora didn't need any more encouragement than that. She did her thing! She let her lips grip and drag from as close as she was to the base of his dick back to the crown of his dickhead. Then she used the tip of her tongue to tickle, tease and excite the tip of his dick for a few seconds.

Then she poured a little Cristal on his dick and hungrily swallowed his dick back into her mouth and sucked and slurped not letting any of the Cristal make a mess in his lap. And as she masterfully sucked his dick in and out of her mouth she held the bottle up with her other hand.

Rambo took the bottle from her hand as he pulled to a stop light on the intersection of Broadway St. and Colfax St. He took a nice swig as the window on the passenger side of the s550 slowly eased down.

He yelled to a homeless guy that stood out on the side walk. When the homeless guy looked, Rambo held the bottle of Cristal up, and without hesitation the homeless guy rushed to the s550.

Rambo reached over and handed him the bottle of Cristal. The guy was ecstatic but more surprised when he looked in the car and seen Aurora's head bobbing up and down in Rambo's lap to the rhythm of "Beyoncé'-Drunken Love".

Rambo nodded and let the window ease back in closing as the light changed green.

Then he rode out and swerved the Colfax St. strip as Aurora continued to enjoy giving him her wonderful wet kisses.

They made it through the smooth but heavy night traffic safely as Aurora intimately and passionately sucked and made love to his dick with her mouth. She looked up at him and asked, "Are we there yet?"

Rambo slowly made a left turn as he softly replied, "Naw ma' it's still kinda early, we still on the Eastside."

She smiled and then looked at his dickhead up close and got real personal with it having a conversation with his dick as she sexily and sultry said, "Yes to you big daddy I like how you control yourself."

Then as Rambo pulled the Benz into a parking space she gave his dickhead a very passionate tongue kiss, and as the whip eased to a stop Aurora looked up at Rambo. He nodded, and said, "That was nice ma', come up for a little air."

Aurora smiled, and then pecked a little kiss on the tip of Rambo's dick, and then pushed and shoved his still hard dick back into his True Religion Jeans. Once she was back sitting up in the passenger seat she pulled the sun visor down and looked herself over.

Rambo looked at her and said, "you still shine bright like a diamond, ma'."

Aurora smiled at him and then whispered, "I can't wait til' you push that big ass dick in me and cut me to a Princess Cut." Rambo smiled.

Then Aurora said, "Real talk babe, I wanna feel the strength and the power of your stroke."

Rambo smiled and readjusted himself putting his still hard woody comfortably in his jeans. At the same time Aurora looked around the area and asked, "Where are we at?"

Rambo shut the powerful v-8 engine off but let the music continue to play as he replied, "This is 17th St. and Franklin St."

Aurora nodded but sarcastically responded, "Well yell, babe. I know that!"

Rambo pointed to small building that was surrounded by a bunch of expensive whips that was parked on the lot. Rambo explained, "This is an exclusive membership only and extremely private high class and high taste club. This is "Club Couples". The members that attend any function here can only come as a couple."

Aurora looked around the s550 for a few seconds, and then she asked, "So are we a couple now?"

Rambo nodded and then whispered, "I am heavily considering what that would be like, but you still have to pass a test at my condo."

Aurora smiled excitedly and said, "A

Feelin' Some Type'a Way

test! I come wit' a college degree and many
other qualities, talents and natural abilities, so
I know I'll pass any test!"

Rambo smiled as they both got out of
the whip and walked the Red Carpeted
entrance, but he said, "Well this is a different
kinda' test…this has nuthin to do wit' school.
You gon' have to be more than impressive on
this test."

Aurora smiled and wrapped herself
around his arm and replied, "Well we just
gon' have to see then, huh!"

Then as they walked through the door
Rambo pulled Aurora even closer to his body
as he noticed how dazzled she was by the
charming and elegant inside of the club. The
hostess stepped to them, and then led them to
an exclusive booth seat. Rambo ordered a
bottle of Dom Perion champagne.

Aurora smiled lightly as she looked
around still captivated by their surroundings
and the people that they were among, but she

whispered, "Babe, I'm lovin' your style…I really must say you are more man than I expected you to be."

Rambo reached across the table and locked his fingers with Aurora's fingers and as he looked deeply in her eyes and communicated with her soul, he said, "Ma' I am so much more than you could think…I'm way more than just a dollar bill…my life is way more than the street tell tales, rumors or secrets, but I would love to encourage and entice you into my life and style."

The waitress brought them their bottle of Dom Perion and disappeared. As Rambo popped the bottle and poured them some glasses of champagne, Aurora asked, "Babe I hope it's not a problem wit' me callin' you babe, I just feel so comfortable wit' it…but anyway, I would love to accept any invitation to share your world."

Rambo passed her a full glass of champagne and said, "again, we toast, ma'."

Aurora smiled a sexy smile as she accepted the glass. They clicked their glasses together as Rambo said, "A couple!" Then they sipped and enjoyed each-others company until the club called for last call for alcohol. Then they left the club wrapped in each-others emotions.

Chapter 6

When Rambo pulled the s550 into the attached garage of his condo he awakened Aurora from her comfortable ride. When she opened her eyes from a comfortable nap she asked, "Is this your condo?" Rambo nodded as he touched the garage door button and closed the garage door.

Aurora smiled and then sexily said, "Now we can see if I can pass your test with flying colors." Rambo just smiled and nodded his head as to say come on as they both got out of the Benz. Aurora followed him as he led the way into the condo.

As soon as they stepped through the door Aurora's expression lit up with excitement as she looked around the condo saying, "Oh babe, this is a beautiful look!"

Then she stepped in the kitchen with Rambo and admired how his kitchen was set up. Rambo pulled out a Vitamin Water from the Sub Zero refrigerator and offered it to Aurora, but she shook her head and said, "I'll share with you." Then she stepped away on her own to investigate.

She passed through the dining room and smiled as she gazed over the dining room table. He had a chess board set up on the table. But the chess pieces were different; they were black prominent people like

Malcolm X, MLK, Noble Drew Ali and so forth. The white pieces were also prominent people such as presidents.

Then she stood in front of the mirror mantle and examined some pictures that lay post there. There were pictures of him by himself, with other females, and pictures of his daughters.

Aurora smacked her tongue and flipped the pictures of him with other females face down, and instead focused all of her attention on the ones of him and his daughters.

Rambo smile at her through the mirror as he watched her looking over the pictures. Aurora looked up and at Rambo through the mirror and asked, "what are we gon' do about these pictures being on display like this?"

Rambo just eased closer behind Aurora and wrapped one of his hands around her waistline and let his fingertips rest and caress her flat but ripped stomach as he replied, "For real, there is nuthin' that could be done about them pictures…these are my precious princess'…they must always stay out front…they're the reason I do it, na-mean."

Aurora nodded as she looked at him through the mirror but she shook her head and softly replied, "No I'm not talkin' about the pretty girls…I'm talkin' about the ugly pictures that I turned face down."

Rambo smiled as he listened to her, but he responded, "Significant suggestions already huh! You still must pass the test before you can start rearranging things!"

Aurora turned around and faced Rambo. She wrapped herself around him and pulled him even closer to her body. Then she looked him in his eyes and reiterated, "The test, huh!"

Rambo smiled, and then leaned down and shared a long awaited but very passionate and intimate tongue kiss. After the kiss Aurora caressed Rambo's chest and down his body. She lowered her body in rhythm with the movements of her hands, but Rambo interrupted her movements and said, "No ma', my precious princess' are here, we gotta take this to the bedroom…my palace."

Aurora nodded and said, "The kingdom is full of girls, huh!" Rambo nodded as he interlocked fingers with Aurora and whispered, "Follow me, ma'."

As they stepped into the living room Aurora was stunned with amazement. She looked around the living room and at the beautiful furniture with excitement and said, "Ooo-wee, now I know you have excellent taste, I love this furniture, babe!" The living room was set up with perfection.

Aurora stood in a daze holding Rambo's hand as he explained the living room, "Yeah ma', that's complicated creations…I designed my own furniture. I picked out my own material the whole 9. The leather is Moroccan leather. I even did the carpet that's underneath the end tables." Aurora nodded as she whispered, "Not just expensive taste, but bomb ass creativity."

Then she walked over and looked out the window at the spectacular view of the mountains and softly replied, "This is a wonderful view, where are we?"

Rambo stepped behind her and said, "Wait until you catch the skyline when the earth rotates this side of the earth back to the Sun in the A.M. and yeah this is the Denver Tech Center."

Aurora nodded and replied, "Nice!"

Then Rambo pulled her hand and pulled her toward the steps and led her up the steps. When they made it to the next level Rambo said, "We're goin' on the third level, this is where my office and my precious princess' are, I need to look in on them, but you can go ahead to the next level."

Aurora pulled him close to her again and wrapped herself tightly around him. She shared another passionate tongue kiss, and after their kiss Aurora whispered close to his ear, "I'll be waitin', babe!"

Rambo nodded and replied, "That's what's up!" Then he as he stepped towards his daughter's bedroom he looked back over his shoulder and as Aurora slowly climbed the stairs he said, "Make yourself at home." She nodded, but continued up the steps making her way to the third level and his bedroom.

Rambo quietly stepped to his daughter's doorway and looked inside. He saw all three of his daughters laid out in their pajamas comfortably in their dreams. He pulled the door closed and smiled as he made his way up the steps to the third floor.

Once Rambo made it to his bedroom he started to feel his body becoming excited and as soon as he stepped into the bedroom door he looked at Aurora's sleepy body as she lay naked across the bed with her curvatious curves silhouetted by the Blue Ray of the 50" plasma TV screen.

He stopped in his tracks and admired her beauty…she was breathtaking! He really felt his adrenaline rushing to his dick…it began to throb with anticipation as he looked at her honey golden well groomed, flawless and elegant appearance lying across the black satin sheets as the goddess she really was.

He quickly reassembled his thoughts as he gazed over the bedroom, but after a few seconds into his gaze he thought to his self, *"She's absolutely the perfect pure essence of what a woman should represent."*

Then he smoothly and quickly moved to the bathroom. He took a quick shower, and then eased next to Aurora in the bed, and as he parlayed in the comforts of his kingdom she rolled even closer to him, and sexily nestled herself into the strong embrace of his arms, letting her body shadow and simulate the likeness of his very own body structure.

They lay nearly the same, wrapped into each other arms the rest of the night… sleeping and finding their minds in a happy heavenly dream.

Chapter 7

Early the next morning Aurora awakened with Rambo's arm still wrapped around her as he slept. She laid absorbing his fragrance and the quiet comforts of his kingdom for a while. That is until she heard the soft whispers of his daughters on the second floor of the condo.

After a few moments of gathering her thoughts and lying next to Rambo she heard his stomach growl with hungriness. She nodded herself with encouragement, and then she quietly eased out of his arms and climbed out of the bed.

She stepped nakedly over to his walk-in closet and surfed through his clothing. She stopped at a few pair of pajama sets, and pulled out an all-black Kenneth Cole silk pajama set.

She held it up to her nostrils and inhaled a deep whiff of his fragrance before she dressed into the silky smooth material. Then she went into his bathroom and looked herself over in the mirror, and then once she was satisfied with her morning appearance she left the bathroom and the bedroom and headed down stairs.

As soon as she declined the steps she noticed one of Rambo's daughters standing in the doorway of their bedroom. Aurora smiled and waved a friendly "hello".

The little girl smiled shyly, but stepped out of the doorway and asked Aurora, "Who are you, and where is my daddy?" Aurora thought quickly to herself, *"This is most definitely a daddy's girl!"*

But she smiled and squatted down so that she was the same height as the little girl and with a friendly expression replied, "Well, your dad is still in bed sleep, and my name is Aurora…What's a pretty little princess like you want me to call you?"

The little girl smiled innocently and sweetly as she softly said, "My name is Ne'va'eh…you can call me Ne'va'eh!"

Aurora smiled and as she nodded she said, "Well I am glad you're woke, cause I'm bout' to cook breakfast, and maybe you can help me prepare your wonderful dad the perfect breakfast in bed!" Ne'va'eh revealed her real smile as her expression really lit up.

Then Aurora asked, "Would you like to help me treat your wonderful dad to somethin' special?" Ne'va'eh nodded with excitement in her face.

Aurora smiled, stood and interlocked her fingers with Ne'va'eh's fingers and as they walked she said, "Come on princess let's make this happen!" Then together they decline to the 1st floor of the condo and made their way to the kitchen.

Aurora opened the refrigerator wide and stood looking at all the food that was inside as she thought about what to cook for breakfast, but then she asked Ne'va'eh, "What's your dad's breakfast food?"

Ne'va'eh smiled with excited eyes as she replied, "French Toast!"

Aurora nodded, and then said, "French Toast it is then."

Ne'va'eh just stood smiling until they heard more laughter on the 2nd floor of the condo. Aurora acted surprised at the sounds of laughter on the 2nd floor, but asked, "Who could that be?"

Ne'va'eh smiled and nodded as she said, "That's my sisters...Cesi and Remy!"

Aurora smiled affectionately as she said, "More princesses' means more French Toast, huh!?!"

Ne'va'eh smiled and said, "I'ma go get them!" Then she turned and disappeared up the first level of steps.

Aurora pulled out the eggs, the butter, the Texas toast, an a little cinnamon. Then as she found a skillet hanging over the center island, Ne'va'eh came back down the steps followed by Cesi and Remy.

As they walked in the kitchen Ne'va'eh's expression presented the biggest and prettiest smile as she said, "Aurora, these are my sisters!"

Cesi sat at the center island on a bar

stool and introduced herself to Aurora, "Hi! My name is CeAjarae, but you can call me Cesi!"

Aurora smiled openly at Cesi and then replied as she extended her hand, "CeAjarae, what a pretty name, but I'll call you Cesi if that's what you like." Cesi smiled a beautiful and friendly smile as she nodded her agreement.

Then Aurora looked at Kareama as she sat at the other end of the island and said, "and you must be, let me guess, you're Remy, huh!"

Kareama smiled and said, "Yes, but my real name is Kareama."

Aurora smiled and replied, "Another pretty name…you all have such beautiful names…so can I call you Remy, too?"

Kareama smiled a real pretty smile as she said, "Yes, you can call me Remy, but your name is Aurora just like the city of

Aurora, and it never sounded so pretty to me until now."

Then Cesi agreed with Remy, "Yeah Aurora is a pretty name to be a person's name."

Then Aurora extended her arms outwards and with a giant, and happy smile that reveal a confidence as she announced, "We all have somethin' in common!"

Ne'va'eh animated and excitedly yelled, "We all have pretty names!" They all laughed and smiled with bright glee in their eyes.

Aurora looked at the stove for a brief moment, and then looked back at the princesses; they all still had happy expressions etched across their faces. Aurora nodded and rubbed her hands together as she smiled and said, "Well the plan is breakfast in bed for y'all's dad, *(then she looked at Ne'va'eh as she said)*and little princess suggested we prepare French toast."

Cesi and Remy both nodded their heads and at the same time they all rhythmically said, "It's our dad's favorite breakfast!"

Aurora smiled and replied, "Aren't we all daddies' little girls!" The girls smiled all identical smiles.

Then Aurora said, "Okay, let's get this surprise breakfast in bed underway before "The King" wakes up." The girls nodded.

Then Aurora started dividing up the responsibilities, and without wasting any time, they had a beautiful breakfast and a wonderful aroma spreading throughout the condo as they carried the breakfast on a tray up the step. Rambo still lay comfortably sleep in his kingdom.

Aurora put a finger to her lips to shhh the girls as they eased quietly into the bedroom. They stood beside the bed quietly watching and holding the breakfast tray of food as Aurora tickled his face with a Rose.

Cesi mumbled happily, "Come on dad, you know it aint no flies in here!"

Rambo smiled a little as he tried to play sleep, but he still opened his eyes slowly and acted like he was just waking up. He peered at his daughters standing with the tray of breakfast.

Then in the perfect harmony Cesi, Remy, Ne'va'eh and Aurora all sang out, "Good morning Daddy!"

Rambo smiled as he faked like he was waking up, and then he winked an eye at Aurora as he sat up in the bed and replied, "All for me!"

Together the girls put the tray onto his lap. Aurora pushed a button on the remote control, giving life to the 50inch plasma screen. Rambo continued to smile and nod as he surveyed the food.

As Rambo looked over everything, Aurora said, "Well we hope you enjoy everything, but we have to go back down stairs and cater to ourselves, and if you need anything just call, I'll come runnin'."

Then the princess' took turns giving their dad Sweet Pieces as they left out of the bedroom. *(Sweet Pieces are daughter to dad kisses.)* Then Aurora shared a very meaningful and intense kiss with him.

Then as she started leaving the bedroom she winked an eye back at Rambo over her shoulder and uttered, "I think I'm passin' the test with flying colors, huh!" Rambo just nodded as she disappeared through the door.

Then as Aurora sat at the island with the little Princess' eating breakfast, Ne'va'eh snatched the breath out of her by asking, "Are you goin' to be my dad's girlfriend?"

Aurora was stunned by the question, totally caught off guard. She was at a loss for words for a brief moment. But she slowly gazed around at the Princess' with a shocked expression. She didn't know exactly how to tell the girls that she just met their dad yesterday, and that she was just tryna see what he's all about.

Then Ne'va'eh smiled and whispered, "Aurora, I like you." Cesi and Remy just nodded their agreement.

Aurora shrugged her shoulders and smiled as she said, "Well we just have to wait and see what y'all's dad think about that ideal, but I must say if the decision was left up to me, I would agree to be your dad's girlfriend…because, not only do I really like him, but I also really like his Precious Princess'!" They all smiled and conversed as they ate until the moment was interrupted by the sound of the doorbell.

Chapter 8

Kareama rushed to answer the door and after she peered through the peep hole she yelled, "Cesi it's your mom!" Cesi's mom name is Leona, but everyone calls her Le-Le.

Kareama unlocked the door, and as soon as Le-le stepped through the door with her upbeat and *Sassy Chic* energy…she smiled, hugged Kareama and sassily said, "Hey Remy, you are so pretty!"

Kareama hugged her in return smiling as she said, "Thank you Ms. Le-le…we're in the kitchen eating breakfast."

Le-le smacked her tongue and sarcastically spoke as she stepped towards the kitchen, "I wonder what aYamp, Slim Pimpin had cook, cause I know he aint did no cooking!" Then as she turned entering into the kitchen her entire energy, body language and facial expression changed.

Cesi smiled and said, "Hi mom!"

Le-le stood looking around the entire kitchen, and at the breakfast, then as her eyes landed on Aurora she spoke to Cesi and Ne'va'eh. She continued to look Aurora over with her vision communicating with her mental faculties. But when she spoke attitude was clearly heard in her voice as she asked, "Where is y'all's daddy?"

Aurora smiled a cynical sneer, and before either of the princess' could respond she answered, "He's upstairs, still in bed."

Le-le's expression instantly revealed her annoyance at Aurora. She stood frowning with a small doddle face at Aurora for a brief moment. Then she turned on her heels and strolled to the steps. She stomp each step with her 6inch Jimmy Choo Red Bottoms as she climbed reaching the third level. When she walked into Rambo's bedroom her voice exploded! Her attitude rocked him right outta the bed.

Rambo jumped from the bed, and as he stood stunned and dismantled he tried to understand what Le-le was so animated and boisterous about. When he finally caught up with her speedy and crafty words, he smacked his tongue and stepped into his bathroom. Le-le stepped behind him with her words still over accelerated as she yelled.

Rambo looked at her through the mirror and asked, "How are you gon try and regulate what goes on at my crib?"

Le-le smacked her tongue again and

continued to yell, "Whenever anything has anything to do with my children I'm gon regulate, and I don't care where I'm at...here, there, aaannnyyywhere, and that's just me!"

Rambo turned and looked her over. Her expression was fueled by her fiery anger. He asked, "Why Le-le? Why are you so angry, what did she do to you?"

Le-le mean mugged Rambo with a real doddle face as she yelled, "She's down there wit' my kids cookin' breakfast...actin' like she's me or somebody else!"

Rambo laughed a little to his self, and then as he stepped pass Le-le back into his bedroom he said, "Le-le, them are my kids, only one is yours, and she is somebody else."

Le-le angrily pushed him across the bed and yelled, "Nigga I don't give a fuck what you're tryna say! Them are my kids too...I'm mother of one and mother to all, just like your other babies mother Traci is mother of one and mother to them all...and I would expect her to raise hell just the same…and as a matter of fact, that's the somebody else I was referring to…let me hit her on her ringtone!"

Rambo laughed even harder when she pulled out her iPhone5 and started texting Ne'va'eh's mom. As soon as Le-le finished texting Aurora calmly and quietly strolled into the bedroom.

Le-le looked at her up and down with an attitude etched across her expression. Aurora just smiled and sat next to Rambo on the bed. He looked at her for a few seconds, and then back to Le-le as viciously mean mugged him with the doddle face.

Aurora softly asked, "Am I really causing this much aggravation, cause if I am, you can take me home…I really am not tryna be a disruption."

Rambo shook his head as he looked and listened to Aurora, and then as he stood up he to Le-le and said, "Le-le for real you know how you are and how you feel, but you gotta still respect me, my lifestyle, and trust my judgments to not just have any kinda female around my children and our daughter."

Le-le smacked her tongue and sarcastically replied, "I've seen the choices you've made in choosing women, and that's why I challenge your judgment's at times." Aurora laughed a little in a low tone.

Then Rambo smiled and said, "That's really not sayin' a lot, cause I choose you too, na-mean."

But before Le-le could respond the doorbell sounded again, and as the doorbell echoed throughout the condo Rambo mumbled, "Let me get this door." Without even responding he walked out of the bedroom leaving Aurora and Le-le in their own company.

As soon as he disappeared Le-le faced Aurora and said, "Well my name is Le-le, and I must apologize because this is really not all about you...his ass has just never had any female around our kids, and me personally, I don't want him to go back to his old ways."

Aurora stood and extended her hand in a hand shake as she replied, "Nice to meet you Le-le, my name is Aurora, and I respect the way you feel about your children. But I must defend myself respectably, I don't know what kinda women he's had in his company in the past, but I am not just any kind of woman...I am my own woman."

Her voice held a quiet force. The sound of her voice revealed her confidence not her cockiness, which helped them to communicate as the women that they really know that they are.

Rambo made it to the first floor of the condo, and as he stepped towards the kitchen he heard his daughter Ne'va'eh's mom laughing in the kitchen with his girls. When Rambo stepped in the kitchen his baby's mom Traci turned and looked at him with a lippy attitude as she replied, "what's this I hear about you havin' a girlfriend?"

Rambo shook his head with a smirk on his expression as he replied, "Don't come in here tryna promote Le-le's psyched out manipulation!"

Traci looked him up and down as she replied, "Psst, child please! I'm not goin' by what she texted me, I'm goin' by what my daughter has just told me, and by the way, where is Le-le?"

Rambo started steppin' into the kitchen towards Traci, but she nonchalantly eased gracefully around the island tapping softly on the girls head saying, "Duck", "Duck", and when she reached the last little head she yelled out "Goose", and took off running up the steps. Rambo just shook his head shaking his attention away from Traci, Le-le, and Aurora.

Then as he opened the Sub Zero and let his eyes travel over everything Ne'va'eh climbed onto his back. She wrapped her arms around his neck and kissed a sweet piece on his cheek, and then said, "Dad all I said is that I like Aurora."

Then as Rambo stood upright and closed the refrigerator door Cesi smiled as she said, "Yeah dad, we all like Aurora, we all think she's pretty…and nice!"

Rambo stood smiling as he looked his daughters over, and as he sat Ne'va'eh back on the bar stool. Then he looked with a blank expression as he said; "Now my Precious Princess' are entangled into this wave of confusion…I wonder how this got started?" They all cracked up laughing.

Then Cesi shrugged her shoulders and said, "I would love to tell you how all this got started, but you used to always tell us to not tattle tale on each-other."

Rambo pulled up a bar stool and sat at the island with his Precious Princess'. He swallowed down some'a Remy's orange juice and then said, "Bae-bae's, first of all, I'm glad to hear that y'all like Aurora, she is nice, huh!?!" They all smiled and nodded as they listened.

Rambo continued, "Y'all only been knowing Aurora for only about couple of hours, but I like the fact that y'all was able to establish o very powerful attraction, but no-one should be able to ever be able to come into y'all's lives and have the power to affect y'all so quick and easy."

Cesi nodded and then said, "Dad it really isn't that easy for us to be influenced, especially by another woman being around you other than our moms…but it's pretty much simple, there has never been a woman here beside our moms. So that's kinda what made us actually think she's influential to you more so than us."

Rambo sat poised and passive as he listened to his daughter's, but his expression was satisfied, and then Ne'va'eh softly said, "It was me daddy! I'm the one that asked

Aurora was she gon be your girlfriend."

Then Remy spoke out, "Yes dad, we never see you with a girlfriend…we think she will be a nice girlfriend for you."

Rambo looked around at the smiling expression that was on his Precious Princess', and then he said, "Since when do dads take advice from his 11, 12, and 13 year old daughters on how to pick a girlfriend!" They all laughed.

Then Rambo looked up at the ceiling as he said, "Thanks Bae-bae's…you girls are most definitely so sweet. Now let me get upstairs and make sure the grown Bae-bae's are not really losin' the best part of their minds." Then he gave each of his Precious Princess' a sweet piece kiss on each of their foreheads, and then disappeared from the kitchen and made his way up to his bedroom.

Chapter 9

As soon as Rambo made it to his bedroom the aroma of marijuana crashed into his face. He shook his head and as he stepped through the doorway Le-le, Traci, and Aurora were all on another level from the effects of the Colorado Kush. They all simultaneously looked at him with beautiful, but intriguing expression.

He shook his head as stepped over and sat next to Aurora on his bed he said, "So as it seems weed calms a savage beast."

Le-le smacked her tongue, rolled her neck, and accepted the blunt from Traci, and after she exhaled a short puff she said, "Well first of all, I'm not a savage or a beast, and the weed aint what calmed me, it was communication. Aurora and I sat up here and let our common sense and our common interest sat us up like the classy women we are!"

Then Rambo looked at Traci, she sat up on his dresser smiling, but she interjected, "Well here's my 2cents…my daughter has her very own intuition, and she's takin' a liking to Aurora, and for the reals, she never really likes anyone…especially anyone getting' close to her dad. So as I said or as I'm sayin', we're parents and if this is who you gon' have in your life I have no problem as long as she will be comfortable around our kids…and just as my daughter I also have a good intuition about her."

Then Traci looked at Aurora and said, "I don't have any problem with you being around my daughter."

Rambo smacked his tongue and said, "Why are y'all doin' this stuff, y'all act like we about to get married!"

Le-le shook her head and replied, "No not married, not that all...we just know if she made it here it must be somethin'...and I told you way back when that I would let you know if I decided to have a man around your daughter, and I expect the same courteous...you know what I'm sayin'"!

Rambo nodded as he looked over Le-le's body as she stepped over and passed the blunt to Aurora, and as Aurora hit the blunt and let the smoke exhale through her nose Rambo asked, "So what time are y'all bringin' my Princess' back over here?"

Le-le answered, "I have a client, but I

most definitely will get them back over here, just call me!" Then he turned his attention towards Traci, She said, "It really don't matter, just call me when you finish makin' your moves."

Rambo nodded, and then relaxed back on the bed. He stared up watching the ceiling fan as it rotated. Aurora stepped to Traci and passed her the blunt, and as she sat back down next to Rambo on the bed lying in complete daze. Aurora asked, "What's on your mind, babe?"

He didn't answer Aurora, but instead he sat back up in the bed smiling. He looked at Le-le and Traci with an uplifted spirit, but at the same time he had a deceptive expression on his face as he said, "I really appreciate this company…but y'all know what I mean, na-mean!"

Traci eased slowly off the dresser and passed the blunt to Le-le, but as she stepped she replied, "Come on Le-le, you know it aint hard to figure out where his mind is at!"

Le-le put the blunt in the ash tray and stood and as she looked at Aurora she said, "Well as it turned out, nice to meet you,' then she looked at Rambo and said, and I'll see you lata' Slim Pimpin'"!

Aurora nodded and replied, "Nice meetin' you, too."

Then all thee of Rambo's Precious Princess' came runnin' into the bedroom as they all listened to Traci's voice echoing through the condo as she yelled, "Nice meetin' you, Aurora!"

Cesi sat next to Rambo while Remy sat on the other side of him. Ne'va'eh forced her was between his legs and sat on his lap. Ne'va'eh softly whispered, "I wanna stay wit' you and Aurora, daddy."

Rambo pecked a little sweet piece on her fore head and said, "I want you to stay too, Bae-Bae, but daddy has to go do some work…but as soon as I finish all of y'all will come right back to me."

Ne'va'eh looked at Aurora and smiled as she asked, "Will you be here when we come back?"

Aurora looked at Rambo. He sat shrugging his shoulders not knowing the answer. Aurora thought to herself, *"Hell yeah I'ma be here! I aint never gon leave this nigga!"* She pulled Ne'va'eh over to her and wrapped her arms around her and whispered, "I sure will!"

Then Rambo said, "Remy you goin' with Cesi, but you're comin' back here too."

Remy smiled. Cesi gave him a sweet piece on his cheek, and said, "See you later dad!" Remy did the exact same thing to his other cheek and said the same thing that Cesi said. Then they took off running out of the bedroom door.

Then Rambo let his attention key in and

focus on Ne'va'eh and Aurora as he said, "Come give daddy a sweet piece cause you know your mother is waitin' on you." As soon as Ne'va'eh's lips touched Rambo's cheek, Traci's voice echoed through the condo again, "Come on Poodie!"

Then as Ne'va'eh sluggishly walked from the room, she said, "Bye-bye Aurora."

Aurora blew a light sweet piece in Ne'va'eh's direction as she walked out the door leaving, and then she looked at Rambo and asked, "Do want me to go lock to door?"

He shook his head and looked at the alarm touch pad on the bedroom's wall…and after a few seconds it began to beep as it flashed a green light that revealed it was armed.

Chapter 10

Aurora looked at the green light on the alarm pad, and then looked at Rambo with hunger in her eyes. She licked her lips tastefully and lustfully with long desire and wantonness. Rambo smiled and nodded because his hunger and desire was identical to hers.

Aurora leaned closer to him and whispered, "Green light means go, babe."

Rambo nodded his agreement, and then pulled her hands and guided her to stand up in front of him as he sat up on the edge of the bed. She eased between his legs as she stood.

He let his hands begin to explore the silk material as he rubbed and caressed every curve on her curvatious body. The silk material wrapped tightly around her body, her hips, and her thighs. As he let his hands explore and discover her sexily built body she slowly and sexily snake charm danced to the rhythm of his firm fingertips.

After a few minutes, he turned her so that she was facing away from him, pajamas bottoms down, then she slowly bent over like a strippa'. Her perfectly curved golden skin lit up Rambo's expression as her powerful, but soft ass cheeks was positioned right in front of his face.

As he continued to ease the pajama

bottoms down her legs he kissed and traced lines and small circles all over her ass cheeks. Aurora twirled her waist to the smooth sensations of his warm breath and moist tongue as she moaned sexy "ahh's".

As they found their own rhythm of togetherness Rambo continued to caress her strong legs on the inside of her thighs toying with her pussy from a different angle as his hands made their way up and down her thighs.

Aurora stepped out of the pajamas and pulled the pajama top over her head. Then she stood in front of Rambo absolutely naked. He rubbed her ass until their hands connected, and then he turned her to the bed and laid her across the silk sheets.

Aurora lay on her back with her legs spread open and inviting. She rubbed herself and caressed herself with one hand while her other hand motioned for Rambo to come to her.

He undressed out of his pajamas and stood looking over her for a moment. Aurora moaned and whimpered, "Come on babe, my pussy is beatin' fast'a than my heartbeat!"

Rambo nodded, licked his lips and stroked his long thick dick, but he whispered, "We got all day ma', don't rush…let me taste your sexy before I get at it."

Aurora hummed at the thought of Rambo putting his warm breath on her hot wet pussy, but she whispered, "Have your way, babe!"

Rambo climbed over her body and kissed her forehead and then he sucked on her moist lips letting her moist lips moisten his lips. Then after a few minutes of that, he started to ease down a little and sucked around her ears and neck stimulating every other sexiness that was in her body.

He let his tongue touch and tingle everything about her as she moaned, "Yes! Yes, do your thing babe!" He did exactly that!

He traced the tip of his tongue between her cleavage, and spent ample amount of time giving the proper attention to each of her full size breast. He sucked and nibbled on each nipple causing Aurora's body to erupt a flow of her love juices and sexy cries of, "more babe, please!" So Rambo gave her more of what she screamed, moaned, and cried for.

He traced the tip of his tongue down the center of her flat but solid stomach, tickling her senses along the way. As his body lowered down her body he found his self at the edge of the bed. He kissed on her belly button and exhaled a warm mist of his breath.

Aurora whispered, "Babe, I really can't believe you!"

Then he eased down a little more until he had his knees on the carpeted floor. He pulled Aurora's body closer to the edge of the bed and kissed little kisses on her beautifully trimmed pussy. He lifted her legs over his shoulders as he continued to tease all of her senses.

Aurora begged and pleaded, "Ooo babe, let me feel your tongue!"

Rambo ignored her and continued to breathe his warm sensual breath on her melting pussy. She started to wind her pussy in little circles as Rambo blew a warm mist of breath into her pussy.

Then unexpectedly he let the tip of his tongue lick up the wetness of her pussy to her clitoris, and as soon as the tip of his tongue landed on her clit she let off an explosion. Her body began to shiver as she yelled out, "Oh babe! It never felt like this!"

She lost all of her self-control. All the cream in her body began to flow. She was all in…Rambo turnt it up even more. The more she yelled, screamed, and creamed the faster he let his tongue tickle her G-spot. She was unable to handle herself any longer. She scratched and pulled at him until he crawled back on top of her body.

His face was soaked with her juices, but she didn't hesitate to lick her own love off his lips and face as she whispered in between kisses and licks, "I don't think you'll ever get rid of me now…you really popped my cherry, babe!"

Without warning, as Aurora spoke he slid his thick long dick into her hot, wet, but tight pussy. They simultaneously let out a sigh of "ahh"! Then as Rambo slowly worked his way in and out of her pussy he whispered, "I already love this pussy, ma'!"

Aurora let out a deep sigh and moaned a deep sigh, "On purpose!"

Then they made love, fucked, and had sex until his cell and house phone began to ring back after back.

After what seemed like an eternity, but was a strong 2 hours of loving and hot fucking, Rambo rolled outta the bed, and as he stepped towards the bathroom Aurora let out a deep sigh and asked, "Do you think I'm like the other females you use to mess wit'?"

He stood in the doorway of the bathroom as he briefly thought about the question. Then he exhaled a deep breath showing that he was speechless with exhaustion, but he shrugged his shoulders helplessly and said, "I don't know the answer to that question, ma', but I do know that there is somethin' real special about you, and I know that I really like it…whatever it is!"

Aurora smiled a sweet and innocent smile as she lay on the bed listening. Rambo stepped into the bathroom, and as he ran some bath water he reflected back on what he had just said to Aurora. He was surprised by his own reaction. He smiled to his self as he reflected on that moment.

Then he turned and looked back over his shoulder as Aurora was stepping into the bathroom. She softly asked, "Can I join you in the tub?"

Rambo softly replied, "I'm actually

runnin' this water for you, and I was gon' ask if I could join you."

Aurora didn't reply but instead, she lowered herself and kissed him playfully, but intimately. She nodded as she started to step into the Jacuzzi tub, an as her feet wadded through the hot steaming water she eased out a sigh, "ahh-perrrfect!"

Then she grabbed Rambo and gently pulled him. He calmly let his body agree with her pulling him, and as he eased into the hot steaming water Aurora whispered in a very seductive voice, "Well babe, now we have the perfect moment…we can really get intimate with one another…you can pick my brain, and I can pick yours…it is so much that I want to learn about you, and I mightiest well start right now that I have your undivided attention."

Rambo nodded his agreement, but replied, "Aye, you so right…I most definitely wanna pick your head apart, but I wanna relax too…so let's just unwind and soak up some'a this good steam and enjoy the calmness of this atmosphere for a few moments." Aurora nodded her agreement.

They both sat in the large Jacuzzi tub and let water wrap them in the comforts of their own thoughts and comforts. Aurora thinking to herself, *"This nigga might be worth more than a hustle!"* Rambo's mind traveled too. He was thinking, *"Aurora is nice!"* But Aurora wrapped her arms tightly around Rambo and kissed the back of his neck as she let her body relax and enjoy the calmness of the atmosphere.

Chapter 11

As Aurora and Rambo sat relaxing in the Jacuzzi tub enjoying the calm atmosphere and listening to the sweet sound of, "Seven Streeter-It won't stop" echoing through the bathroom's surround sound, Aurora whispered, "That must be our song…because we keep hearing it, and plus, you are making me feel some type'a way."

Rambo said, "Then that'll be our song forever, huh."

Aurora started to message Rambo's shoulder for a few moments, and then she leaned up pressing her hard nipples against his back as she kissed and sucked his ear lobe...then she turned his face so she could look into his deep brown eyes as she whispered, "I can really envision that forever you're speakin' about."

Rambo looked into her eyes, her face and studied her a little until she kissed what wasted on his nose and cheeks. Then she said, "the youngest Princess Ne'va'eh asked me am I gon' be your girlfriend."

Rambo maintained a solid face not giving her nothin to read as he read her, but after a short moment he asked, "So what was your answer? Cause I can see how she's attracted to you as well...which is absolutely shocking to me...I've never seen her open up and relax to no one other than her mom so easy, and that's being gentle because at times she's not even open to her."

Aurora smiled, and then said, "Babe it's a woman thing…you wouldn't understand." They both laughed a little.

Then Rambo asked again, "So what did you tell her or how did you explain…or better yet decorate your lie?"

Aurora smiled, as her mind remembered what she had said to Ne'va'eh, and then she said, "Since you must know! I actually said, that we will have to wait and see what you think about that idea."

Rambo nodded, and softly replied, "That's actually a good way not to say a thing, huh!"

Aurora splashed a little water on Rambo's face and made a sound of "Psst!" and then she said, "But I also put some icing on the cake too…I told her as well as Cesi and Remy that if it was left up to me I would agree to be your girlfriend, because I really like you, and that I also like your precious princesses…and that ain't no lie, no fabrication, no decoration-just the flat out truth and nothing but truth. So how you like that there, Mr. Man?"

Rambo shrugged his shoulders and nodded his agreement but as he sat thinking for a brief moment, Aurora kissed his ear and quietly asked, "What's on your mind, babe?"

Rambo remained quiet in his thoughts for a few seconds, but when he had caught up with his mind he said, "I think you got me really feelin' some type'a way... I think you just might be that Diamond in the Ruff".

Aurora nodded and then said, "I am most definitely a good woman, and I am most definitely looking or should I say, holding onto myself until I find the right guy or again should I say my perfect soul mate….and I must honesty admit, ever since I met you I've been feeling some type'a way too….and that's wit knowing that you're a Mangy Dog!" They both laughed together.

Then Aurora asked "What did you think of me at first sight?"

Rambo laughed lightly to himself, Aurora smiled, but punched him softly, and then asked, "What's so funny babe?"

Rambo peeped back at Aurora. Her gaze was full of question and her expression held suspense. She paid very close attention to what Rambo might say. She was unable to escape her awareness and her anticipation. She push Rambo and with a serious and forceful demeanor, she asked again, "What did you think babe, for real!?"

Rambo nodded as he discreetly smiled, but he replied, "Look ma," then he looked Aurora in her eyes. He was able to read her soul and her emotions. So he knew he couldn't keep it 100 with her. He knew he couldn't just come and flat out tell her the truth. He knew the truth would hurt her.

Break her heart. He knew that he couldn't just come out and say he wanted to see how her fuck game was or if she had a good head game.

So he did what his game would allow him to do. He maneuvered. He said, "It's what it was….I felt some type'a way on sight… I felt like a little kid riding in the back seat of the car with my parents playing that's my car." Aurora smiled because she played the little game also.

He continued, "Cause as soon as you and Poetry bent the block you caught all of my attention… I was next to my homie and yelled out to my Nigga, "That's my Bitch" and excuse my French but I was just speaking English."

Aurora nodded and said, "I understand the term Bitch, and I personally have a bomb knowledge of self. I know who and what I am, and I most definitely know when I'm being a Bitch or not …. But you can go on."

Rambo nodded and then continued, "Yeah as I was saying, I basically chose you on sight. I wasn't getting at you for just a little hump, naw that wasn't what was up. My instinct told me right out that gate that you was the one…and I survive off my instincts most of the time, because I pay attention to me and what goes on in my mind. So I must have a bomb knowledge of self too, Huh!"

Aurora smiled a soft smile as she nodded her agreement. Then Rambo raised up and hit the spout so the water could drain. Then as he stood he helped Aurora to her feet, and said, "We can go in there and take a shower." He pointed to the shower.

She followed him to the shower and they stepped in, and shower together, cleaned each other's everybody part. When they stepped from the shower and dried themselves off, Rambo asked, "What did you think about me? You know you kind 'a, had some kind' a frown on your face when you and Poetry stepped in my space."

104

Aurora turned back and rolled her neck and said, "Your space!" She smacked her tongue as she put that same frown back on her face and replied, "I do believe that was Juneteenth's space. I didn't see any booth with your name on it."

Rambo nodded a little and replied, "See Ma, that's cause once you seen my face you lost your focus and if you would have paid more attention to detail you would have seen my booth right in front of you...the one where they sold The Urban Fiction Books."

Aurora looked questionable as she reflected back on the moment and then she said, "You're the author. You write books." Then she thought for a second and smiled then she remembered Poetry saying her homeboy was a writer. She smiled "That's you Huh!"

Rambo smacked his tongue and tossed his towel over her head and walked out of the bathroom. Then as Aurora stepped out of the bathroom and started getting dressed Rambo asked again, "What did you think about me?"

Aurora smiled, and Rambo smiled sarcastically and said "Aw now it's your turn to find a joke within yourself."

Aurora just laughed lightly to herself, and then she said, "You know how I felt about you right out the gate...that was pretty obvious."

Rambo shook his head and said, "It couldn't have been that obvious, I still had to put in work on the block and at the mall."

As Aurora looked at herself in the mirror she looked at Rambo through the mirror and winked her eye and replied, "How you think you woulda felt if you didn't have to do work for what you wanted." Rambo smiled as he nodded his agreement but the whole time he watch and stared at Aurora's curvaceous round ass.

She peeped how he was hypnotize by

her curves so she played with him and his attention. She wiggled her ass sexy to the rhythm of "Rhianna's Shine Bright Like a Diamond" as it played through the speakers. Rambo shook his head and his mind back into the moment. He looked at her through the mirror. She winked an eye at him again, and then said, "Don't let me find out that you're only dazzled by the booty."

Rambo smiled, then said "Psst, never that! I just speak booty and I like the way your booty talk!" Aurora smiled, and then she asked, "Can Poetry come pick me up here…you know I left her with my Range Rover."

He nodded then stood looking at himself in the full body mirror making sure he was fresh as he meant to be, as well as making sure he removed all the tags from his clothing. He told her the address as she called Poetry. After a short call with Poetry, Aurora stood and wrapped herself around Rambo as he sprayed on his Gucci Cologne.

She rubbed the spray into his Gucci button up short sleeve shirt and asked "What time can I come back to you?"

Rambo shrugged his shoulders and said, "You still got that line…let me call you when I get home." She smiled then he said, "Let's go downstairs…I gotta get a few things ready for my ride out."

Aurora just nodded but as she followed him down the steps, she mumbled sadly, "Will you *please* miss me while you're gone!"

Rambo nodded as he descended the steps, but he replied, "as much as you miss me." As Rambo gathered some things together the doorbell sounded. Aurora looked sadly at him because she knew that was Poetry. Rambo yelled through the door, "Here she comes!"

Aurora walked to him and wrapped herself around him. She whispered, "I don't wanna go, Babe."

Rambo replied, "I don't want you to go, but the sooner you go, the sooner you can get back to us."

Aurora back peddled as she pulled away. She looked ashamed and lost in love, and as she opened the door Rambo said, "I'll call you."

Aurora whined, "You promise!"

Rambo nodded and said, "I Promise You!"

Then he watched her glide gracefully to the driver side of the Range Rover. When she pulled off he smiled to himself and whispered as he close the door, "Got me feelin' some type'a way for real."

Chapter 12

Aurora pulled the Range Rover into Poetry's apartment complex and parked in front of Poetry's apartment as she listened to Poetry explain her night at the club and her morning after. Aurora smiled at how Poetry exaggerated every detail about how niggas were tryna get at her.

Poetry is a beautiful chocolate sister. She also has the look of a Queen, an Egyptian Queen. She has a smooth Hershey chocolate skin complexion with jet black hair, and a curvatious but slender tall body...over all she's a beautiful young woman.

Once Aurora had the SUV parked Poetry was tire of hearing her own voice and story, so she looked at Aurora with a mean mugg expression and tried to speak as if she was a gangsta as she said, "Enough about me, bitch tell me about tour night with the world class D-Boi, Rambo!"

Aurora smiled brightly at the mentioning of Rambo's name. Then Poetry leaned back against the passenger side door with a very skeptical look on her face as she said, "Un-un bitch! No you aint!"

Aurora gripped the steering wheel of the Range Rover and as she nodded her head widely she yelled, "Yes bitch, yes I am! I think he's that nigga!" Poetry nodded and high fived Aurora.

Then Aurora looked at Poetry with the seriousness of a killer and said, "Bitch, I don't know any mutha fucka but Romeo and Juliet that fell in love this fast…but it ain't just me that's head over these Red Bottom Heels…his ass is all the way open too, and to top it off, I met his everything…. I met his daughters, and Bitch he has some very beautiful little girls and they really genuinely like me."

Poetry smiled and nodded as she listened. Aurora said, "I even met his baby's moms." Poetry's expression quickly changed to a frown.

But Aurora quickly stop her attitude as she replied, "Un-Un Bitch it ain't like that…Oh don't get me wrong, when they first came in and seen me posted with his silk pajamas on, that probably one of them bought for him, their attitude was all over the place. The shit was kinda funny but you know me. I held my composure."

Poetry rolled her neck and the ghetto flowed right out of her. She said "Psst! Bitch I woulda laughed right in them Bitches face, Crunch!" They both laughed loudly.

Then Aurora features soften and she said, "Naw Bitch, it really didn't turn out like that. It almost did, but it didn't. We ended up smoking some bomb together."

Poetry looked shocked and surprised, and then quickly said, "Yeah Bitch one of his BM's fired up a blunt of some kill …but I knew it was all good because the baby's moms are cool. I think the only real thing was I was sitting in the kitchen eating breakfast with the daughters, and his daughters had never seen the Big Bad Dog with any females besides their moms."

Poetry nodded and replied, "Yeah well Rambo does know how to play it Huh."

Aurora just nodded her agreement as her mind quickly strayed off into her own fantasy world. But she subconsciously spoke "Yeah he does know how to play for the Reals."

Poetry sat quiet as she watched how happiness and the first signs of a love jones exuded from Aurora's characteristics. Poetry just shook her head and whispered "Yo ass done fell in love wit the world famous D. Boi, Rambo."

Aurora smiled, and then replied, No Bitch he's not a D. Boi, He's D. Man!" They laughed again.

Then Poetry asked, "Well this really ain't none of my business, but did he get his money's worth?" Aurora looked kinda confused.

Then Poetry said, "You know bitch, he spent about 2 Racs ($2,000) remember...did he get about a rac worth of pussy out yo ass?"

Aurora answered in the most sultry voice that she could come up with as she said,

"Well bitch, if this wasn't that important, I would tell you everything, and I mean from the size of his long, thick, juicy and tasty dick...all the way to how he licked and got his face wet." Poetry smiled lustfully as she listened.

Then Aurora crushed her moment and her nosy appetite with, "But I can't tell you that...I'm way too much of a lady to be letting you know what goes on in between the sheet, na-mean!"

Aurora smiled and laughed while Poetry's expression held a frown. Poetry smacked her teeth and tongue and said, "Aw Bitch gone on with that love on the first night shit"

Aurora revved up the power engine in the Range Rover but she said, "Bitch, I really don't know what this is. Yes love is a very, very powerful word and I really don't play around with that it, but that Nigga, that guy, no that Man has got me really feelin' some type'a way."

They sat staring at each other briefly, and then Aurora asked in a calm and quiet voice, "Have you ever made love to a man, and I'm not talkin' just fuckin a Nigga...I mean letting a man into you're everything…into your heart, into your soul. He touched my body in a way that it has never been touched."

Tears flowed down her cheeks, down her smooth golden skin as she spoke, "It was like it was my very first time. He showed me what it really means to pop a Bitch's Cherry…to give him my virginity, and we know I was not a virgin but actually I was, cause I never love that much, especially not for real. I gave him my heart, body, and soul willingly. I gave him my love."

As Poetry sat listening her eyes overflowed also. Tears streamed down her smooth chocolate cheeks. She whispered, "Aurora that's real, that's how love 'pose to happen …you didn't go in there and try to make love happen. It just happened…love made you happen like that…that's what's up. I can't knock that, girl you do your thing. You make that man feel you and you keep feelin' that man cause you never know how shit might unfold."

Aurora reached over and wiped the tears away from Poetry's face as she nodded her agreement. Then Poetry smiled and said,

"Girl I'm so happy for you, for real! I'm happy for Rambo too. He needs a bad Bitch in his life. He needs to stop wasting his time and goodness on getting at Colorado CooChii that's just tryna play wit this emotions, money & time."

Aurora nodded and then as she pulled the seal belt around her body and got comfortable in the driver's seat, and said, "I'm most definitely a bad bitch but bad meaning good and well girl you know how they say it, you gotta play the cards you're dealt, and it looks like I got a good hand. So I'ma play this wit' caution, care and concern and if this thing really unfolds into somethin' special, bless me and if it does not I'ma just flow day by day but most of all girl, I'ma just let this do what it's doin' because for real, it's making me feel real good, na-mean."

Poetry nodded, and then they shared a hug. Then Poetry eased out of the Range Rover. She said, "Call me Girl!" Aurora smiled and nodded as the door slammed shut. Then poetry stepped back and watched Aurora as she rode out in the Range Rover Sport.

Chapter 13

As Rambo rode throughout the city in the black on black S550, the day was a perfect Friday. The blue sky was cloudless, the sun had what looked like the perfect picture setting on top of the Rocky Mountains, and you know as always the air was clear and Colorado clean. Rambo let the power and luxurious whip gracefully glide across the Colfax St. strip.

He kept his attention focus on the fast pace traffic, but at the same time he had his eyes peeled on all the activity, schemes and what not-that went on up and down the sidewalks on the Colfax St. strip. The sidewalks were crowed with low grade drug dealers, $20 Hookers, and every kind of base heads, dope fiend, meth monster and just any kind of evil demon alive.

Once Rambo seen the person he was in search for, he pulled the glamorous whip to the side of the street. A nigga on the sidewalk face looked up as soon as he noticed the big power pretty and smooth whip pull to a halt. The nigga waited until Rambo stepped out on the driver side and he said, "What's up Hog?"

Rambo nodded as he stepped over and leaned back against the wall, and then he softly said "What's the business like on this end Messy?"

"Messy" is the homeboy from the Southside of St. Louis. He hustles hard. His game is information, he knows somethin' about anyone that's doing just about anything. Messy shrugged his shoulders and shook his head with a grin, as he said, "You know how it is on the strip Hog…bad work and hard work unless you gotta slick bitch on the flirt, and a nigga like me ain't got neither one, so you know I'm just standing around looking like a jerk." They both laughed.

Then Rambo pulled a fat bank roll outta his pocket and tossed it to Messy. Messy caught the bank roll outta the air and looked suspicious. Rambo nodded his head one time and whispered "That's a $800 blessing, but what I need is to know somethin' about this bad chick, her name is Aurora…and that's all I know for now, but get at me, there's more where that comes from but you gotta be fast and furious or I'll gain the knowledge before you, and you'll miss out on getting mo-bread, na-mean."

Messy nodded and tucked the bank roll away, and then Rambo stepped back towards the driver side of the whip, but before he ease back in the seat he said, "I still hustle hard but hustle smart and got the same ringtone so get at me as soon as you get that information, na-mean."

Messy nodded, and then turned and disappeared around the corner. Rambo revved the power but quiet engine back up.

He looked out at the speedy traffic until he caught an opening to ride in. Then he rode out with the Colfax St. traffic.

As he drove he called his cellphone, the iPhone5 that Aurora has. She answered on the first ring. Rambo smiled as soon as he heard Aurora's sultry voice,   she said, "Hello, Hello!"

Rambo said, "Hey what's up Ma', are you missing me as much as I'm missin' you?"

She replied, "Stop it, stop it babe, you know I'm missin you. I'm so glad you call."

Rambo pulled to a stop light on Quebec St. and Colfax St. and as he sat at the red light he asked, "What are you doin?"

Aurora wanted to lie and say nothing, but she said, "On my way in, I stopped at Barnes and Nobles and picked up one of your books, "Ready in the Game," and I've been sitting here trapped in the story."

Rambo laughed and then said, "I'm on my way to this happy hour in the hood…you wanna come and sit next to me?"

She quickly answered with an enthusiastic, "Yes"!

Rambo nodded as he pulled away from the light and as he drove he said, "It's an old school joint, but it's the joint. It's on 40th and Steel St…how long will it take you to get there?"

Aurora said, "I'm on my way, I'll be there in 20 minutes."

Rambo smiled and then said, "Aw-ight, but you drive safe."

Aurora happily said, "Okay Babe!" Then she clicked off the line.

Within minutes Rambo was pulling the beautiful black S550 on to Mr. A's parking lot. The parking lot was crackin'. It was the perfect time of the day. Everyone with jobs was just getting off work and coming to the bar to officialize the weekend and continue the Juneteenth celebration.

Rambo sat outside his whip nodding, waving and sharing dapps with people as they continued coming and going from the bar. Then he noticed Aurora in the white on white Range Rover Sport. He walked over to her SUV as she parked and waited for her to climb out of the big SUV.

As soon as he laid eyes on her, he smiled and talked to his self, *"damn she's nice."* Aurora was fresh. She had on some form fitting DKNY jeans that accentuated every curve on her body. She had a white DKNY half T-shirt that revealed a clear cut diamond in the belly ring. Her hair was in a different style. She wore the Shirley Temple Curls; the one's that only Snoop Dogg was able to get away with.

She shook a curl out of her face and revealed her beauty. Her total package was standing on a pair of blue Jimmy Choo red bottom stilettos. She was absolutely bad. She looked up and noticed Rambo standing there waiting. She smiled and stepped towards him with a graceful tope. As soon as she reached him she wrapped her arms around him and whispered, "Hey babe," and as they hugged he kissed her on her cheek. She turned his head and kissed him on the lips.

Then she whispered, "Babe kiss my lips, I wanna taste your breath every time." He nodded then their hands automatically connected as he said, "Come Ma, let's go have a couple drinks and soak up some'a this happy hour." Aurora held his hand tightly and walked beside him every little step he took.

When they stepped inside the door of the bar and seen the crowd and how live it was Rambo smiled. Aurora looked around curious and very concern. She's never been in this part of the hood. She's been downtown and on the Eastside, but she had never been inside of function that was this packed and rocking with black people.

She wrapped her arm even tighter around Rambo's arm and pulled herself even closer to him. He turned a little and focused his gaze at her. She smiled innocently. Then he nodded and eased to the bar with her as close to him as she could get.

When he reached the bar, he held up two fingers. The bartender nodded and then brought two shot glasses and a bottle of XO Remy and poured two double shots. Rambo broke bread with the bartender and passed Aurora a shot glass as he snatched up his shot glass. He said, "Drink that slow Ma' that's a real drink!"

She nodded and took a sip, and after she let the strong Congac slide down her throat. She said, "Oh, babe this is strong…What is it?"

Rambo took a nice swallow and said "This is Remy XO, the Taste of Class."

Aurora took another sip, then she turned

the shot glass up and drunk the Congac.
Rambo shook his head as he looked at the
frown Aurora had on her face after she
knocked the drink off.

Then she leaned closer to Rambo and
wrapped her arm around his waist as she said,
"It was strong as hell, babe, but I rather knock
it off cause I prefer to hold you instead of that
shot glass."

Rambo winked an eye and replied,
"That's why I called you, cause I rather you
hold me too." She smiled then Rambo
downed his drink and as he wrapped an arm
around her he pulled her close to his body ad
held her close to himself as they rocked
slowly to the rhythm of "Kelly Rowland's-
Motivation."

Aurora looked delighted to be in his
arms. She fit very comfortable in his embrace
and as they moved well and in sync together,
Rambo said, "I'ma give you the key and
alarm code to my condo, I need to go pick up
my precious princesses. I'll meet you there."

Aurora nodded then Rambo said, "You
can go grab you a change of clothes if you
like."

She smiled brilliantly and rocked her

head and replied, "I'm two steps ahead of you…I brought me a set of clothing. But I prefer to keep wearing you silk PJ's, and I love the way they fit on me and I love the fragrance of you that's in the material."

Rambo nodded and replied, "That's that then, let's get in traffic, I know my Bae-Bae's are waiting."

Aurora nodded with a smile and then followed Rambo as he led her out of the bar and to her Range Rover Sport. She wrapped her arms around him and shared a long passionate kiss, and after their kiss Rambo let her climb in the SUV and revved it up. Then he pushed the door close and said, "Make yourself at home".

She smiled a sweet smile and said, "Fo-Sho, Babe!"

Then Rambo stepped over to his Mercedes Benz, and eased behind the steering wheel. He revved up the powerful AMG engine and followed Aurora's Range Rover off the parking lot. Then he went on his way to pick up Cesi, Remy and Ne'va'eh…his Precious Princess's.

Chapter 14

Rambo pulled into his driveway…he pushed the button on his garage door opener, and as the garage door raised they all seen a white Range Rover Sport. Cesi asked,

"Dad you bought me a Range Rover?"

Rambo smiled as he shut the engine off, but he replied, "Not yet Bae-Bae, that's Aurora's whip."

When Ne'va'eh heard Aurora's name she sang out loud, "Yayyy!"

Rambo turned and smiled at Ne'va'eh and said, "That's your home girl, huh!" Ne'va'eh smiled and nodded as they all climbed out of the car.

As soon as they stepped in the condo they was soaked up by the smooth sounds of "Jaheim's-Put that Woman First", playing on the surround sound as their nostrils were mesmerized by the buttery aroma of movie Theatre popcorn.

Ne'va'eh walked right over and stood next to Aurora in the kitchen. Aurora smiled down to her with a happy smile and asked, "How are you princess' doin today?" Ne'va'eh just smiled.

127

Kareama smiled and replied, "Hey Aurora, I'm good, how are you doin' today?" Aurora smiled at Kareama and responded, "oh, I am lovely today thanks to your dad. He's just been so nice and sweet to me."

Then Cesi smiled and sarcastically asked, "When you gon let me drive my Range Rover?" Aurora acted like she was looking for the key. When she couldn't locate it she smiled, and with a serious tone she said, "When I find the key Cesi, you can take your sisters for the ride of y'all's life!" They all laughed with happiness.

Then as Rambo looked around the kitchen and through his Sub Zero refrigerator he mumbled, "Don't tell her that, she still has three more years before she's even able to sit behind the steering wheel of any kind of whip." Kareama then add her input, "and I have four more years, and I want a Benz like you dad." Rambo smiled and nodded, and then looked at Kareama and Cesi, and said, "You girls have expensive taste, I just wonder who's planting those thoughts in the little minds of yours."

Then he looked at Ne'va'eh and asked, "So in five more years, what kind of whip you want? Ne'va'eh looked shy with her expression, but she said, "I want a black Barbie corvette or I'ma just ride with you and Aurora everywhere."

Rambo looked at Aurora then Aurora softly whispered, "We're at least gon last for five more years."

She smiled discreetly then passed the bowl of popcorn to Ne'va'eh. The girls all walked in the living room and stood around sharing popcorn and watching the movie Planted of the Apes as it was on the preview screen.

Once the girls was out of ear shot Aurora stood in front of Rambo and wrapped herself around him and whispered, "I missed you Babe" He kissed her forehead and down the bridge of her nose until his lips touched her lips sending shocking waves lengths throughout her body. As they kissed she hummed, and then after their display of affection, she moan, "Oh Babe you taste so good to me!"

Rambo gave her a breezy smile and nodded. Then he asked "What's on the big screen?" Aurora stepped back and said, "Take a guess"

As she gave him hints like they were playing sharaids. She acted like a monkey. Rambo smacked his tongue and said, "Oh that's so easy, The Planet of the Apes."

She smiled and stated, "I was thinkin maybe you and I and the girls could have a movie night. I ordered Pizza already."

Rambo nodded as understanding gleamed into his eye's, but then he said, "The girls have movies in their room, they can't watch The Planet of the Apes cause if they do, guess what's gon' happen."

Aurora nodded her understanding, and then replied, "Someone's gon' make me scoot over in the kingdom, Huh?"

He nodded and said, "Yes, your new best friend."

Then Rambo looked to the girls and said, "You can take that popcorn to y'all's room and watch the movie up there." They took off without any respond and as they climbed the steps Rambo yelled, "Y'all know I don't like it when you make a mess."

They yelled back, we won't make a mess dad."

Then Aurora yelled, "I'ma bring y'all a pizza." Then Rambo said, "Come on ma' let's go in here and watch your family on the silver screen."

Aurora frowned and tried to punch Rambo, but he was already running towards the living room. When she caught up with him she said, "Them apes' aren't my family babe, but then again, when they're mad, that's just how my people are sometimes…drunk, crazy, and insane."

Rambo sat in the lazy boy recliner and pulled Aurora on his lap. She hit the play button on the remote and let the DVD start. As the movie started playing, Aurora concentrated on the screen letting Rambo study her. His mind wanted to explore her mind. Without turning to look at him she asked, "What's on your mind Babe? I can feel your thoughts."

Rambo licked his lips as he caress Aurora's curves through the soft silk material, but he said, "That's cause we have a bomb ass harmony. We really feel each other."

Aurora kissed his forehead and as she smiled she replied, "I know, Huh!" He nodded, and then he continued, "I got a real question for you. Don't think I'm strange or anything for asking. I just wanna know its natural curiosity, Na-mean." She looked very attentive as she nodded her agreement. Then Rambo looked deep into her honey golden eyes and asked, "Have you ever been in love before? And I ain't talking about that mushy ass Valentine's day thing… I'm talking about what Mary J. Blige was talking about…. A Real love."

She sat for a brief moment and let her brain appraise the question. As she thought about the questions Rambo let his eyes and his third eye (his mind) measure her and her sincerity. Then she slowly shrugged her shoulders and softly, but her voice carried the intensity of a sincere person as she said, "Well I thought I was once before. It was somethin', but I later came to the realization that it was absolutely not love. Don't get me wrong it was somethin' and somethin' cool, but it just wasn't somethin' that woulda been able to take me to the next level."

Rambo continued to look her deeply in her soul, but he asked, "What's the next level?"

133

Aurora returned the same look to Rambo that he gave to her, and then she looked deep in his eyes into his soul, and as she looked deep in him she saw something that made her mind accelerate. She saw love! Her pretty face burned. It melted. It went soft as silk. She was unable to take her eyes, her attention and her emotion off of him. As she stared in his face she softy and sexily said, "Babe you know the next level of love and relation is marriage. Have you ever been married before?"

He felt he could step outside of himself. He felt he really trust her already. He felt completely comfortable talkin to her. He looked ashamed and disgraceful trying to put it in words, but he said, "To make it simple and to the point…I once was married, but my behavior was disgraceful…I was absolutely not a cooperating participant."

Aurora smiled slyly and repeated, "Not a cooperating participant, what a good way to say a cheater, huh!"

Rambo shrugged his shoulders and sunk his chin in his chest, but Aurora lifted his chin and rebooted his confidence as she said, "That was in the past, babe…get over that, at least you learned somethin' from that experience…that's what's meant by growin' through adolescence…you'll never grow through a thing until you add lessons in your life, and that's just life, babe."

Rambo smiled a little and pulled Aurora close to his body. He wrapped himself completely around her. Aurora felt great in his arms; she let out a soft sigh, "Ahh!"

Then Rambo said, "I've never told anyone these things…keepin' it 100 about that, has never happen before…now I know I'm feelin' some type'a way!"

Aurora smiled and whispered, "It's alright, babe, I told you I feel the same, and whatever happens, I want it to happen!"

Rambo softly and calmly replied, "Right before our eyes Love is happening."

135

Aurora kissed him on his lips and whispered, "On purpose!"

Then Ne'va'eh called over the loft to Aurora and asked about the pizza. Aurora continued to kiss Rambo again and again, but in between kisses she spoke to Ne'va'eh saying, "I'm-on-my-way-little-princess!"

Then Aurora raced to the kitchen. She snatched the pizza and as she raced back past Rambo blowing him a kiss as she race up the steps to Ne'va'eh with an entire pizza. As soon as she made it up the steps Ne'va'eh asked, "Can you hang up here with us for a while?"

Aurora smiled a friendly smile, and then she spoke over the loft to Rambo, "It's girls time, I'll see you in a lil bit." Rambo nodded, and then reclined back in his Lazy Boy and relaxed in his own thoughts and emotion until he nodded out.

Chapter 15

About 20 minutes after Rambo nodded off, he was awakened by the sound of his doorbell ringing. His eyes popped open with a questionable expression on his face, but he got up to answer the door.

As he stepped in front of the door's peephole he regained his full awareness before he looked out and after he looked, he moved his head back and stood with a look of shock. He let his mind wander for a moment, and then he shrugged his shoulders, unlocked and opened the door. It was Poetry.

As Rambo stood in the doorway he asked, "Did Aurora call you or somethin'?"

Poetry looked up at him with a serious expression. She seemed uptight and very nervous. Rambo could see somethin' was wrong with her.

She replied, "No Bo she didn't call me, I came on my own…I wanna talk to you, I don't know what's happening wit' me, but I know it's because of you."

Rambo stood in the doorway looking confused as he said, "Poetry I don't have company at my crib…you shouldn't be here, let me get Aurora to explain this to you."

Before he could push the door close Poetry stopped him, she softly but seriously said, "I didn't come here to talk to her…I need to talk to you."

Rambo looked back over his shoulder for a second, and then as he stepped out the door he pulled it close behind him. Then he looked at Poetry as serious as he could look. She looked serious also, but her seriousness wasn't a look of seriousness as Rambo's was. She just looked different. She was not her normal self.

Rambo softly whispered, "What's wrong, Poetry?"

She shrugged her shoulders and frowned a little to soften the impression, but she whispered, "It's you! I know you and Aurora are trying to do whatever it is that y'all are doin', but I think you and I should have a thing or at least try somethin' out…I like you too, Bo…I've been feelin' you. Yes, as a friend and a homeboy, but ever since that day at the mall I've been feelin' some type'a way. I know you are really startin' to feel

Aurora, but I can't explain this feelin'…I mean, all I know is that I'm tryna get with you Bo!"

A glimpse of anger crawled across his expression as he stood staring at Poetry. He shook his head slowly, and as his head shook, tears started to slowly stream down Poetry smooth chocolate skin. Poetry whined, "Don't turn me down Bo, you have to see how I am…you have to see how I am…how I love…how I'm really a good woman for my man."

Rambo's anger was apparent as he fiercely asked, "Well why don't you have a man already! Cause you full of shit, na-mean! You should not have come here…this shit is all wrong. Your integrity is way too messy… (*Poetry just stood with tears pouring down her face as Rambo tore into her character.*)

"You have a lot of nerve coming to my condo without me inviting you here…you have a lot of nerve tryna intrude and invade on me and Aurora's happiness. What kinda friend would even have that kinda nerve to take that kinda leap away from a friend? That's just way too shifty of a behavior for someone that still considers them self a friend."

Poetry shook her head frantically as she reached out and tried to touch Rambo, but he pushed her away. She tried to speak, but not a word came from her mouth. Her voice was gone! Her voice didn't agree with her emotions or her thoughts. She was punch drunk after absorbing Rambo's assault on her character and her intentions.

Rambo continued to let his anger loose, he said, "Please! Poetry don't be an itch, I'm beggin' you Poetry, don't mess this up like you have already messed up your friendship with Aurora...I'm beggin', please don't!"

Then Poetry replied, "Bo, I'm beggin' you too...what about me...you won't even take the way I'm feelin' into consideration...I have feelings too…what about me, Bo, I'm feelin' some type'a way, too…what am I pose to do, not care about the way I feel…and just be unhappy cause I can't have what I want?"

Rambo shook his head and as he stared at her his anger boiled over completely. His expression crumbled into a frown as his voice exploded, "Bitch yo-shit is throwed! Yo-shit is all wrong! Backwards! And twisted! I'm beggin you, not to be such a fool…you act like we're crashin' yo-party, yo-happiness, yo-desires…but you're the intruder…you're the prowler that's trying to intrude and invade on Aurora's happiness, on my happiness…

What about you, there is nuthin about you! There is nuthin I can do about your feelings…I have no reason what so ever to take yo-feelings into consideration, and if you're unhappy it is really not my fault, you're in control of your own happiness and unhappiness, and from what it looks like, you're real good at creating your own unhappiness…and once again I beg you to not ever, and I mean EVER, come here again. Please listen to me Poetry, please!"

She stood with anger, envy, and jealousy etched across her face as she listened. Rambo continued, "I value my feelings so if you value your life as much as I value my feelings, I would advise you, no, I beg you to not fuck wit'em, na-mean!"

Poetry smiled a smirk and then smacked her tongue, and said, "Rambo, nigga I'm just tryna fuck you and fuck wit you…but I really aint the bitch for you to be tryna scream out idle threats to, you really don't wanna fuck wit me the wrong way, na-mea!" Then she smiled and turned, and as she stepped she said, "We'll see who gets the last laugh."

Rambo stood and watched her as she walked away from the condo. Poetry yelled back, "Oh yeah, and if you don't keep this between me and you, I won't keep this address between us, na-mean!" Then she laughed as she disappeared around the corner of the parking lot.

Rambo just shook his head with mad rage. He stepped back in through the door and slammed it as he stormed pass the kitchen.

Aurora and the girls was in the kitchen popping some more popcorn. They all noticed his anger. Ne'va'eh put her hands over her mouth and whispered, "OOO-wee, dad's mad...somebody's in trouble!"

Cesi stood behind Ne'va'eh just nodding her head in agreement, but Remy took off behind him. She caught up with him in the living room, and sat on the arm rest next to him on the Lazy Boy.

She interlocked fingers with him and whispered, "Dad whatever it is, it will be alright."

Rambo nodded and smiled lightly at Remy as he let her beautiful smile eased and soothed his emotional disruption. His anger quickly evaporated. He pulled Remy onto his lap…he hugged and planted sweet pieces all over her face as he replied, "Thank you, Bae-Bae! I needed that for sure…keep havin' my back, for real."

As he held Remy, Cesi, Ne'va'eh, and Aurora came into the living room with the freshly popped popcorn. They all crowded around Rambo and shared in the moment of happiness, and as Rambo sat with his Precious Princess' and his new found favorite girl, happiness once again bubbled back into his heart.

They all sat in the living room and enjoyed each other's company the rest of the night until it was time to shut everything down and relax in the comforts of the Kingdom.

Chapter 16

The next day, June 21st Saturday afternoon, actually the first day of summer, and who knew the heat and the intensity of emotions would be so turnt up. Rambo left the s550 parked in the garage. He and his Precious Princess' rode with Aurora in her Range Rover.

As they all rode his daughters sang along with the music as it slapped through her system. Rambo directed Aurora on how to get where they were going, and within a short period they were pulling up in front of Cesi's mom's house. There was a nice size family kick back. The girls were happy to be there…they were ready as ever to play and eat some good Bar-B-Que.

Aurora watched the girls as they got excited to be getting out the Range Rover, but Aurora said, "Y'all wait, I want a hug…I'ma miss you girls!" Then she hurried from the driver side to the sidewalk and started hugging all the Precious Princess'. They told her how much fun they had with her and that they would miss her too.

The only thing that was different was when Remy whispered to Aurora, "Please take of my dad!"

Aurora returned a bright smile to Remy along with a questionable expression, but she whispered, "Don't worry little Princess, he's the best hands outside of yours…mine!" Remy smiled and nodded understandingly as she accepted Aurora's reply. Then she smiled, nodded, and then ran and caught with her sisters.

Aurora wrapped herself around Rambo in a very intimate embrace for a long moment, and after their show of passion Aurora stepped back a little and asked, "Do I really need to ask you to please miss me?"

Rambo made a cool expression as he shook his head and replied, "Naw ma', you aint gotta tell me…I know I will…you just make sure you miss me when you're gone!"

Aurora smiled and said, "Aw-babe you know I already miss you, and I aint even gone yet."

They hugged again for a long moment, until Curtis, Cesi's older brother yelled, "Yeah she's pretty Bo, but you don't have to get mushy on the sidewalk!"

Then Cesi's older sister hollered from the back yard, "Yeah, get a room, Bo!" They all laughed.

Then Rambo nodded his head once and said, "As a matter of fact, turn the Range Rover off, you can kick back here wit' me!"

Aurora gave a look of disagreement as she asked, "Are you sure, babe?"

Rambo nodded and replied, "I'm absolutely positive, and if you can't stay, neither will I."

Aurora reached into the Range Rover and shut the engine off. She handed him the key and said, "Here, I'm with you, babe."

Rambo nodded and then called Ladeshane', Cesi's sister and introduced her. Ladeshane' grabbed Aurora's hand and said, "Come Aurora, all the girls are all out back." Aurora smiled, but she followed Ladeshane' to the back yard.

Rambo stepped up to Curtis as Curtis was dribbling the basketball. Curtis smiled and said, "Look at you man, Are you in love or are you crazy?"

149

Rambo smiled and said, "Aw-lil pimp you worried about more than your lil fertile mind can handle, na-mean!"

Curtis shrugged his shoulders and said, "I'm just sayin', you know how my mom is…she's gon' tear into this moment, but they already say that your heart might be on anther cloud…you know word around here is the only thing that's fast'a than the speed of light."

Rambo laughed a little, then Curtis smiled and looked over his shoulder and then back at Rambo and said, "But me personally, today I think it might be craziness, more so than love." Rambo laughed as he turned and walked in the front door of the house.

As soon as Rambo walked into the living room it got quiet in the kitchen. He smiled as he thought about what Curtis said, because he knew whatever they were talking about, it was about him.

He stepped into the kitchen and spoke to

Le-le and her friends. Le-le didn't waste a moment, she let her attitude and her fiery personality explode out of her element as she said, "How are you gon' just bring your little friend over my mu-fuckin house…what made you even think I was gon' be cool with *that!?!"*

Rambo smiled coyly at Le-le friends as he absorbed everything that she said. He held his composure together. Le-le's friends gathered their things together as one of them said, "Le-le we're out back wit' everybody else, cause y'all need to talk about this among y'all selves." Le-le nodded to her friends as they exited out the back doorway.

Then as she started putting some seasoning on some ribs she mumbled her emotions as Rambo stepped behind her and tried to calm her down. But she brushed him away. He smiled and sat up on the kitchen counter and asked, "so fo-real really Le-le, what's the problem…you don't want me…let me be comfortable wit' someone else."

151

Le-le looked over her shoulder at Rambo briefly. There was really no emotions in her eyes, but she said, "not only did you bring your yamp, excuse me…cause she hasn't even shown me that she's a yamp, *yet*…but not only do you bring her over without tellin' or askin' me, but she doesn't even have the common cou8rtesy to come in and speak."

Rambo smiled and as he shrugged his shoulders he said, "It aint even like that, Le-le!"

Le-le smacked her tongue, and then Rambo asked, "Le-le, what's really the problem?"

She turned quickly to face him. The first thing that caught Rambo's attention was Le-le's eyes. They were flooded and ready to over flow, but she whined, "I love when you come by…I love being able to talk with you the way I do…I feel that won't be possible…our ability to go head to head will be takin' away."

Rambo sat with a look of confusion on his expression as he asked, "Why, why would you not be able to say whatever's on your mind…you're doin' that right now aren't you?"

Tears started to flow down her beautiful caramel complexion. Rambo tried to wipe away her tears as best as he could, but they continued to flow. Le-le pointed to the back yard and yelled, "Because you brought *her* over here!"

Rambo shook his head and replied, "Aw ma' that's my work or my new woman for now, and I feel she should be a part of whatever I'm a part of, na-mean."

Le-le shook her head and tried to wipe the tears from her face as she adjusted her attitude. Then Rambo said, "don't be like that ma'…we pose to really understand each-other, especially as parents, na-mean."

Le-le nodded and replied, "Yeah I understand that, but for some reason, and I don't know why, but I'm feelin' some type'a way…I don't know why I'm even tellin' you this, but it is what it is…I been feelin' this way ever since I came over and seen her in your kitchen with my girls! You know I can't really put this shit in words, but I know it's love, and I understand that love has its own language for its own listeners…but don't get me wrong, I aint tryna cock block or short stop what you're doin', but don't forget about me…don't forget about your daughters mom."

Rambo smiled as he thought to his self, *"my daughter's mom."* But before he could respond the back door swung open, it was Ladeshane with Aurora. Ladeshane smiled and excitedly said, "Bo, your girlfriend is *soooo* cool, for the reals!"

Aurora smiled a friendly smile as she spoke to Le-le. Le-le manufactured a smile and said, "Hey girl, I hope you enjoy yourself, and don't mind my family…I know at times they can say and do the most."

Aurora smiled and wrapped her arm around Rambo's arm as she replied, "Oh it's all good, every family has its own ways, it already seems happier than my own family."

Then Rambo interrupted their conversation and said, "Enough of this stuff, let's get outside and do what this kick back all about…let's be one big happy family!" They all nodded their agreement and went to the back yard with the rest of the family and friends and enjoyed themselves.

Chapter 17

After the kick back Rambo climbed behind the steering wheel of the Range Rover. Aurora rode the passenger seat as Ne'va'eh and Remy sat in the backseats. As Rambo drove his Princess' fell asleep with their seat belts snugged tightly around their bodies.

Aurora leaned over and kissed Rambo softly on the side of his face, and then as she sat back in the passenger seat she said, "I'm so glad you asked me to stay at the kick

back…I really enjoyed everyone and myself."
Rambo just nodded as he drove.

Then Aurora said, "I didn't want to
cause or create any confusion, babe…it
turned out real cool…Le-le is so cool, huh!?!"
Rambo just nodded again without showing
any emotions.

Aurora could see that there was a
problem with him, she asked, "Is everything
alright, babe…you seem kinda upset and
uninterested?!?"

That is exactly how he felt, but he
replied, "Everything is good ma', I just tend
to get caught up in my thoughts at times, its
nothin'."

Then Aurora smiled with great
enthusiasm as she asked, "Well can I ask you
something?"

Rambo looked back at the girls…they
were good in their dreams. Then as he looked
back to Aurora he replied, "Yeah, what's

up?"

Aurora leaned back against the passenger side door and asked, "Who were you in love with?"

Rambo looked at her with a puzzled stare for a few seconds, and then she asked, "Which one of your children's mother were you in love with, or were you in love with them all?"

He nodded and then whispered to his self, "in love with."

But before he could answer the question he pulled in front of Remy's mother's house, and woke Remy, and when she looked up he said, "You're at home Bae-Bae."

Remy smiled and as she gathered her things she asked, "When are you gon' come back and get me?"

Rambo smiled, because he didn't know the answer, but he said, "Bae-Bae just stay ready…it could be any day…just know for sure that I am gon' come back and get you, aw-ight."

Remy smiled, nodded and replied, "Alright dad."

Then as she climbed out of the back seat she said, "Bye Aurora, and tell Ne'va'eh that I said bye."

Aurora let the window down on the passenger side and said, "Bye Remy and I'll see you soon...I promise."

When Remy made it to the front door it swung open and quickly closed shut behind her. Aurora smiled as she turned in her seat. She softly but sarcastically said, "Well I know who's mom you were *not* in love with!" They both laughed.

Then as Rambo drove through the Green Valley Ranch neighborhood he said, "Well she was cool, but that was then, and after that she was really not for me, na-mean."

Aurora nodded and replied, "Yeah I know what you mean, because some people are only just that, cool!"

Rambo nodded and pulled the Range Rover in front of Ne'va'eh's mother and aunt sitting on the front porch smoking a blunt. Aurora let down the window on the passenger side and yelled to Traci, "Hey girl!"

Traci smiled and yelled back, "What's up Aurora, come hit the grass."

Rambo was turned around in the back seat getting Ne'va'eh's attention, and as soon as Ne'va'eh was aware she said, "I wanna stay at your house, daddy!" Then she put her mean face on.

But Rambo smiled and said, "I know Bae-Bae, but you have to spend some time with your mom, too."

Aurora peer at Rambo and said, "I'm on the porch." Then she eased out of the Range Rover. She went and sat with Traci and her

160

sister Meka. Rambo finally got Ne'va'eh to agree to go home. They walked slowly up the driveway, and as Ne'va'eh pulled her dad's hand, she pulled him through the doorway. As they eased through the door Aurora said, "Bye-bye Ne'va'eh. I'll see you soon, okay!" Ne'va'eh nodded.

Traci shook her head and said, "Y'all bring her back to me with that St. Louis attitude, mean mugs and shoulder shrugs!" They all laughed.

Then Traci stood from her seat and said, "Here Aurora, you can sit here…I gotta go calm Poodie and welcome her back home." Then Traci disappeared into the house.

Rambo sat on the sofa with Ne'va'eh trying to cheer her up, but when Traci walked into the living room she looked at Ne'va'eh the way only a mother can look at her child and said, "I know we don't need an attitude adjustment!"

Ne'va'eh kissed a sweet piece on the

side of her dad's face, and then got up and stomped off to her bedroom. Rambo smiled as he watched her storming off.

Then Traci let her attention land on him. She smiled as she asked, "So as for you Mr. why haven't you called me?"

Rambo looked at her with a confused look and then he replied, "Called you, what do you mean?"

Traci sat next to him on the sofa, but this time her voice had a feminine whine in it as she said, "We'll you use to call me at least once a day or once a night, but now that you have somethin' new or somethin' else to do…you don't have no time for me no more, huh!"

Rambo smiled and then whispered, "What is this, do I detect a little jealousy?"

Traci smiled and got smart as she replied, "You're not a detective, so you must not be detecting what you think you are detecting…it's most definitely not jealousy…it's somethin' all the way different!"

Rambo looked at her as he listened. The light from the moon light illuminated Traci's features. He let his mind speak out loud subconsciously, "Damn Traci, you look really good, what have been doin' to your skin?"

Traci smack her tongue and snapped, "Nigga don't come wit' that bull-shit! Because, if I look so good, why you wit' other bitches?"

Rambo quickly tried to shhh her, and then he said, "Come on now with that bull-shit…you aint tryna be my work!"

Traci stood defiantly with her hands firmly posted on her hips in a very intense stance as she replied, "When did we ever officially break up…we've had our up's and downs, but I still consider you my go to guy…I know how we've been, but yo-ass is still mine…don't make me get G.H.E.T.T.O."

Rambo shook his head and replied, "Traci you know I love you, for real!!!" Traci nodded as she listened. He continued, "But I don't know that you love me...well maybe you do love me, but I know you don't love me the way I would want you to love me."

Then Traci smartly said, "But I can though, you know I can!"

Rambo stepped in front of her as he stood and said, "Babe, maybe you can, but ever since you chose Mr. Wrong your mind and your emotions has been crisscrossed."

Traci leaned back on her legs and rolled her neck and snapped, "And who the fuck is Mr. Wrong?"

Rambo smiled and whispered, "Oh you need his last name, huh! Well his first name is Mr. Wrong and his last name is Decision!"

Traci laughed, but Rambo was so serious, and as he walked pass her he said, "Well I gotta get!"

Traci grabbed his arm and whined, "I still love you, babe, I really do…I just got myself caught in a situation that I should have been stepped away from…but whatever the case, it won't stop me from feelin' some type'a way…I even think I love you even more, now."

Rambo shook his head and as he stepped he said, "When I think you really took the time to learn what love really is we goin continue this conversation." Traci frowned her expression up and tried to pout. But Rambo said, "Don't be tryna look like Ne'va'eh…she's the only one that can make me move with that look."

Then he declined the steps and stepped back out on the front porch with Aurora and Meka. Meka smiled softly looking high as she asked, "When are you gon bring me a copy of your new book "Ready in the Game", Aurora was just tellin' me how she's so trapped in the story."

Rambo reached his hand out and helped Aurora stand as he reached out. They interlocked fingers as they stood next to each-other. But Rambo said, "Meka, it's on Amazon...it's easy to get, even if you don't wanna leave the crib, or you can just go to Barnes and Noble...just go grab it so you can be Ready in the Game, too!" Rambo smiled.

Meka smiled, and replied, "I'ma get it...Aurora has my mind and my interest peeked." Then they all said their goodbyes.

As Rambo and Aurora eased off in the Range Rover Traci stepped back on the porch with tears piling up in her eyes, Meka asked, "What's wrong Traci?"

The tears exploded from her eyes and raced down her smooth chocolate skin as she cried out, "He don't love me no-more!"

Meka rolled her neck and smacked her tongue as she said, "Girl please! Bo gon' love you for-ever...you just see him with that girl, and now you feelin some type'a way."

Traci shook her head as she watched the Range Rover driving out of her sights, and then she whined, "but he aint gon love me the way he really pose to love me…the way he really loves when he loves."

Chapter 18

As Rambo drove the Range Rover leaving Green Valley Ranch Aurora asked, "So babe, which one was it that you loved…was it Cesi's mom or Ne'va'eh's mom?"

Rambo Looked at Aurora with mild interest, as he softly repeated, "In love with."

Then Aurora smiled with a hint of humor as she asked, "Babe what's wrong, you seem to lose apart of yourself every time you drop off one of your daughters."

Rambo nodded and replied, "Yeah ma', my Bae-Bae's always makes me feel some type'a way when they go home."

Aurora nodded her understanding, and then she replied, "Babe you have a beautiful smile, and I have the sense that you don't smile enough."

When Rambo pulled to a red light he relaxed back in the seat in his own mind until the light change back green, But when he drove off, he said, "You show do have a lot of questions, ma'!"

Aurora smiled and shrugged her shoulders and replied, "Babe, I just wanna know you, about you, and what makes you really tick…besides the fact, I got know somethin' about the person I'm getting' involved with, huh."

Rambo nodded as he drove, but Aurora continued to whip her game, "You're very interesting to me…I don't really understand men like you, complicated men."

After a brief moment of thought Rambo asked, "So what's there to know, and what makes me so complicated?"

Aurora shrugged her shoulders and answered, "I just think, why do you not have a woman, I mean you have a lot goin for yourself…you're not into bullshit. Why is a good man single, especially with baby moms that are so close in your life…but that's that, I just wanna know you, your love, and your previous love." Then Aurora sat with a smile froze on her face as she waited on his response.

Rambo pulled the Range Rover to a small park off Tower Rd. in the city of

Aurora, and as they stepped outside of the whip Rambo walked with Aurora beside him, and as they sat on a park bench he said, "Well first of all, let me tell you about my love...I use to really love Traci and a couple of other females...I know how, but it was happening probably in my own mind.

"But anyways, let me continue, Le-le was a really cool female to me, but now I do love her as my daughter's mom, and that's my previous loves...everything else you gotta find out on your own."

Aurora wrapped herself around his arm and snugged closely to him and asked another question, "Well babe, what happen to your love with her, your love with Traci?"

Rambo squeezed Aurora's arm tight in his embrace as he thought for a moment. Aurora broke his concentration because she said, "Babe I just wanna know so I will know how to love you the right way, but if you're uncomfortable with this we don't have to talk about this."

Rambo nodded and exhaled a deep breath and said, "Well ma' it was pretty much the same…things just kinda fell off…I think we just kinda fell outta love…we had our good moments and our bad moments, but shit just came to an end."

Aurora laughed lightly, and then apologized for her laughter as she replied, "Babe it's really not funny, but you basically said the dream was over."

Rambo laughed a little, and then said, "Yeah, huh! Cause that's exactly what happen...it was a good dream, but the dream is over…but I must admit, we still do have a good friendship as a mother and a father,."

Aurora nodded as she listened and then she replied, "Yes, I can see that you and her have a bomb chemistry, and that's very nice for the sake of Ne'va'eh."

Rambo nodded, and then Aurora looked

up into the sky. Rambo's eyes followed her eyes and looked up into the sky also as Aurora said, "The night sky is amazing; it tells a beautiful story about life."

Rambo whispered as he looked up above, "Yes, I like looking into the heavens."

Aurora shook her head and replied, "No babe that's not heaven…the sky is not heaven…it is our universe, and Earth is a part of the great big universe."

Rambo looked at Aurora with gentleness, she nodded and continued, "For real babe, no can explain what heaven looks like, but through a powerful microscope one can explain the universe and the galaxies."

Rambo shook his head and softly asked, "Where you get this information from, ma', and what kinda beautiful does the sky tell right now?"

Aurora stood up happily and pulled Rambo off the park bench, and as she pulled him and stepped she pointed to the sky and said, "Look babe!" Then she described the course of the stars with her finger, and as she pointed up she said, "See that big formation of stars, that's the Big Dipper…that's a male energy. It's one of the more powerful enlightments of the male gods."

They continued to step slowly through the damp grass as Aurora continued to outline the course of the stats, but then she pointed to the Little Dipper, and then asked, "That's the Little Dipper. Do you know what energy that is?"

Rambo nodded as he replied, "I guess that would have to be the female, huh!"

Aurora smiled nodded, and when she let her arm ease around his waist as she said, "It will really never be a beautiful sky without them both being visible…it's just like a beautiful family…one with both energies; male and female…father and mother."

Rambo smacked his tongue and said,

"Sounds good, but where you come up with this stuff, ma'?"

Aurora looked serious as she softly said, "Babe its science, and science is just the way somethin' is studied."

Rambo looked at her with a questionable glimpse, and as she looked back at him she had an enthusiastic expression on her face as she said, "For the reals babe, it could be true and at the same time it has a chance that it could not be true…but if you study and make it work for you, then it's all good…just like I'm doin' wit you…I'm asking you the right kinda questions…studying you so that I will know how to learn you, make love with you, and be the best I can be for you. It's all a science in making two energies exist together…I'ma make sure that I learn you so that I can love correctly, and forever…remember!"

Rambo looked at her with serious eyes for a moment, and then he said, "Enough about this and that…it's my turn to learn and know about your love and previous love." Then he asked, "Who was it that you were in love with?"

Aurora smiled, turned and wrapped herself tightly around Rambo. They tumbled down to the grass with Aurora landing on top of him. She kissed him softly and sweetly on his lips and said, "I've been waitin' on you to ask me that, but anyways, I wasn't in love…not like I thought I was! He was a professional bull-shitter. He made everything in the semblance of love, but he was just tryna mirror a relationship he already had…he had me all the way fooled from the gate. He had me move to Las Vegas thinkin' we was gon have this happiness, when all the while he was still livin' in Cali doin his family thing. His job had him in Vegas at least 4 day a week, but I was just on standby so he could have some pussy and a place to call home when he was in Vegas…"

"When I found out about his fake ass, I

went to Cali and knocked on his door. I
apologized to his wife and told her how full
of shit his ass was and always will be. She
thanked me, filed for divorce, and took his ass
for everything he had…the house, whips, and
I don't know how much money she cashed
out with, but she found out about the Range
Rover and told me to keep it, especially since
it wasn't my fault. I really didn't want it, but
oh well it was for me anyway."

"But yeah, he was a big time nigga in
the casino world…but like I told you babe, all
the time I had with him thinkin' I was in
love…all the good times I had wit' him still
don't make me feel as good as I feel when
I'm with you."

Rambo wrapped his arms around her
and shared a very passionate tongue kiss.
They share their most intimate moment. Their
bodies grinded into each other's bodies loving
each other's movements and reactions. They
touched and kissed each other everywhere.
They stared in one another's eyes as their

faces and expressions were illuminated by the golden light of the moon. After they rolled sexily staying in touch with the moment, they collapsed with exhaustion and pleasure.

Then Rambo whispered, "Let's get up and get to my Kingdom so we can really love what we do to each other." Aurora smiled as they both got up and lovingly and gracefully walked back to the Range Rover.

As Rambo revved up the powerful engine he gazed at Aurora' delicate, but elegant features and whispered, "I don't wanna call this love and then be disappointed...so I will say I have a genuine affection for you."

Aurora sat listening with a trace of confidence as she whispered back to him, "Babe, you can call this whatever you want too...I feel it too, and I might can't tell you what heaven looks like, but this absolutely feels like heaven."

Rambo nodded and as he drove to his

condo they both sat quietly and all consumed in their own thoughts about one another…and this is feelin' some type'a way…and this is Love."

Chapter 19

The next day Sunday morning started off just as beautiful as the night before had ended. Rambo woke up with Aurora wrapped tightly around his body. He inhale the beautiful fragrance of Aurora's hair as she lay comfortable on his chest. As his body expanded from inhaling and exhaling Aurora hummed and sighed as she pecked small kisses in his chest. She use the tip of her tongue to tickle and toy with his chest nipples as he let his senses explore her aroma.

Rambo whispered, "Last night was bomb, ma'!" Aurora continued to let her tongue lick and tease his chest with affection as she whispered, "I know, huh! We have a bomb rhythm together, but relax babe let me wake you up with a sunshine on this sunny Sunday morning."

Then he watched her as she let the tip of her tongue glide and trace a warm breath line down and across his strong and powerful stomach until she had her lips nestled at the crown of his dickhead. She kissed and sucked on the crown of his dick very passionate and with expertise, making squirm all around the bed. Aurora stopped long enough to moan, "Relax babe, and don't hold back from me!"

Rambo let out a loud sigh, "Mmm!" Then he whispered, "Let me have you at the same time!"

Aurora smiled, but she rearranged her body on the bed and positioned herself so that her pussy's wetness was at his lip and easy for him to get to, all the while she was still sucking and swallowing in as much of his long thick chocolate dick that her mouth. As she let his dick ease to the back of her throat, he traced the tip of his tongue up and down the warm wetness of her pussy.

He squeezed her ass cheeks and rotated her ass as if he was screwing her pussy down on his tongue. She continued to kiss and suck the full length of his dick as she skillfully displayed her determination trying to reach a sense of accomplishment.

Rambo licked and made pussy sucking noises as he did all he could to match and keep up with her suckin' and slurpin'. They licked and sucked each-other rhythmically until they both reach the delights of loud sighs and never before reached ecstasy. Rambo grunted and "mmm" his delights, as Aurora's delicious sex flowed through his lips and all over his taste buds and down his throat…and at the same time Aurora hungrily bobbed her head and gripped her lips tightly around the thickness of his dick sucking and moaning with great pleasure as she tastefully swallowed every drop of his flavorable love not any get amount slip back out of her mouth.

When Aurora realized how sensitive Rambo was becoming to the touch of her tongue she slowly and carefully raised her head so that his thick soft meat eased from the grips of her beautiful lips. She looked back at him as he continued to suck and savor the delicious and tasty juices that continued to ooze and drip onto his tongue. She sexily said, "Mmm babe, you got me flowin'so much!"

Rambo replied, "Yeah ma', and you taste real good…I'm still chasin' your waterfall."

Aurora smiled and rocked her hips sexily and hummed as she replied, "And I love the way you chase it!"

Then Rambo tapped a stinging smack on her ass cheek Aurora climbed up off of him. She repositioned herself and kissed his face and lips making sure that she cleaned her love off of his face, and as she hummed her delights she said, "Babe, I think we've been struck by Cupid's Bow, because everything we do is absolutely perfect for us."

Rambo nodded, and replied, "Un-huh!"

Aurora climbed out of the bed and gracefully glided her curvatious body towards the bathroom. Rambo sat up on the edge of the bed and reflected in his own mind. He heard himself speak out loud, *"I've never tried to find love, how is this happening?"*

Aurora peeked her head back out of the bathroom door as the water filed up in the large Jacuzzi tub, but she asked, "Why are you questioning this, babe…you should just go wit' the flow…this is love…if this is really what it is, it will create its own flow, all we gotta do is let it do what it's doin'!"

Rambo just nodded, but Aurora smiled and continued, "Don't be afraid of failing, babe, especially when you're succeeding with everything that you're doin."

Rambo listened very attentive, but his eyes were full of uncertainty and fear as he shrugged his shoulders.

Then Aurora stepped back over to him, she lifted his chin and whispered, "Babe you're a lover...everything you've done to me was with love...don't be scared of your emotions...they're very strong, but you gotta stay in harmony with your heart. You can't let your previous mental wounds interfere with your present pleasures and desires."

Rambo nodded and kissed Aurora's diamond belly ring, and then said, "Ma', I'm just being me...doin' what I do. I'ma Libra, I question myself, because I know I need to be sure that I'm doin' the right thing, don't get me wrong though, everything about you feels righter than a mu-fucka...and what I've seen

185

thus far…I'm really liking, but I've been fooled before, and I promise you I don't want this heaven to turn into an ugly dark nightmare."

Aurora pecked a kiss on his forehead and as she turned and headed back to the bathroom, but she said, "Babe, this situation is goin' beyond what is usual," but before she closed the door her face revealed a trace of arrogance as she let a smile leap upon her face…but she continued, "besides babe, I aint gon let you down…you already got my heart in your pocket!" Then she closed the door behind herself.

Rambo sat staring blankly at the bathroom door a he nodded a careless confidence, then he thought to his self for a few moments, and then after he gathered his thoughts and emotions he stood and stepped to the bathroom, but as he stepped he mumbled, "I think she just might be worth the struggles, the frustrations, and the pains that might be an unlikely possibility."

When he stepped through the bathroom door Aurora was soaking in the bubble bath filled tub. She smiled and said, "I've been waitin on you to join me…next time babe, don't make me wait so long."

Rambo nodded, and then eased into the tub with Aurora. They enjoyed one another's comforts in the steaming hot tub as the soothing sounds of Alicia Keys rocked through the surround sound system.

Chapter 20

Later on in the day Rambo pulled the s550 into the Red Lobster's parking lot, and parked next to Aurora's Range Rover Sport. She stood at the doorway of the restaurant as Rambo approached her. She was beautiful; everything about her looked as if she was glowing. She stood smiling as she waited on Rambo to step to her. She showed so much confidence about herself as she patiently waited on Rambo.

Rambo let a smile trace his expression as he said, "Aye ma'…you're lookin'

Her smile lit up even brighter as she wrapped herself around him, but she softly thanked him, and then pulled his hand as she turned and entered the restaurant. Rambo just stepped and followed her through the entrance. The hostess smiled as they entered.

Aurora smiled in return to her and said, "We're ready to be seated."

Once they were seated at their table Aurora ordered and spoke in the perfect language about the kind of food and how she wanted everything to be. Rambo's attention was fixed on her, but his mind was appraising her mannerism, her voice, and her confidence. His mind whispered, *"Everything is different about her, she holds all of my attention. I aint never met this kinda woman!"*

Aurora smiled at him and asked, "What's wrong, babe, you look like you're in a trance?"

He shrugged his shoulders a little and as he nodded, he replied, "I was, huh!"

Aurora took a sip water and then asked, "What's on your mind, babe…if I do anything that you're feelin' let me know, for the real, you have to, how else will I know that I'm making you feel some type'a way."

Rambo slowly shook his head, and said, "Naw ma' that's most definitely not what it is…I'm feelin' everything about you …your voice, mannerisms…I've never really dealt with the kinda woman you are…and for some reason you seem to be more woman than what a woman is supposed to be, and I really feel like I've met somethin', no, I mean someone very right!"

Aurora smiled casually as she listened to him express his feelings, but the waitress stepped to their table and placed a Chef's salad and Ranch dressing in front of both of them, and then disappeared.

Once the waitress was gone Aurora's mind assembled her game as she replied, "Yes babe, I'm glad you feel that way about me, and I must say in being honest, I enjoy you and your company…I really , enjoy the fact that I can just be me, be myself. I don't have to be some phony bourgeois broad, and that alone made me enjoy this entire weekend with you…and I would absolutely love to have more of you and your time. I know in this what, about 72 hours I've had the best hours in my life…."

Then she smiled and looked real business like and serious as she said, "And I know you can do a lot better…and I want more!" Then her expression quickly returned back into a smile. Rambo nodded his agreement. Then Aurora looked at the Chef's salad and licked her lips and said, "Let's dig in." They continued talking while they ate. Aurora explained how she enjoyed everything about him.

When Rambo finished his salad, he said, "For real ma', this whole feelin' is somethin' different for me, it's good and I want to keep feelin' this way…and we seem to be strongly attracted to each other, but if we gon make any attempt to keep this flow, we gon have to be 100 wit' each other…we seem to be feelin some type'a way, but what's just as important as havin' a strong powerful love?"

Aurora pushed what was left of the salad away from her gently and as she sat relaxed and comfortable she replied, "Trust babe! We have to have a trust that is impossible to penetrate!" Rambo looked real serious as he nodded his agreement.

Aurora recognized how his expression had transformed. Because, even though she sat back poised and confident, she still was very attentive to his mood, she said, "I know how to trust babe, but I haven't found anyone until now, that I would want to put my all, my everything, my trust into…before now the only person I've actually trusted outside of my parents is my friend Poetry."

Rambo's hand instantly raised from the table and quieted her to a hush whisper. The deepness of his voice lowered to the sound of a baritone. His angry expression revealed the seriousness of his mind as he said "Poetry isn't anyone's friend, and in bringing her name up…that's what and who I want to speak about."

Aurora broke into the conversation with a half-smile as she said, "What's up? What's wrong with Poetry? She actually said that she was happy for us…that she was happy for you."

Rambo shook his head and softly said, "Well ma anyone can make their mouth say anything, but when you pay closer attention to detail and mannerism you'll start to learn serious character flaws about anyone or anything we, all have them." The conversation came to a stand-still because the waitress appeared at the table with their dinner.

After their food was placed the waitress disappeared, Aurora expression showed a hint of frustration as she stared blankly at him. His expression was calm and confident as he continued, "This is not merely quality gossip, nor am I trying to assassinate anyone's character, but the reason I say Poetry is not anyone friend, is because she understands our happiness from whatever you shared with her and now she working as a snake. She's tried to go behind your back and get at me... back biting and back stabbing a friend is one of the worse betrayal of all."

Aurora attitude became obvious. Her anger held her speechless. She sat motionless as her mind stared in its own ruthless imagination. She really didn't want to believe what she was hearing. She shook her head angrily and softly whispered, "No not Poetry...not my home girl!"

Rambo spoke the absolute truth. He looked into Aurora golden brown eyes he could see that she was unstable and that she was puzzled. Her gaze was   questionable. Her foundation was disturbed she slowly shook her head again and again as she said "No not Poetry...I just find that hard to believe!"

Rambo looked straight into Aurora's emotional eyes as they filled with tears, and calmly said, "No lie! That night you went upstairs with pizza and my Precious Princess'."

Aurora's calmness quickly disappeared, the tears poured right from her eyes as she said, "That's who was at the door that night?"

Rambo nodded as he noticed a sense of panic on her expression. She looked around and mumbled, "Where is the restroom?"

Before Rambo could respond she had snatched up her Louis Vuitton bag and was out of her seat. He watched her as she walked away, he carefully looked at her profile as she stepped. He felt something stir within as he held his attention on her. When she pushed into the ladies room door Rambo leaned back in his seat.

He talked about everything in his soul;

he questioned himself about *"whether or not if he should have mentioned this."* Then after being drenched in his own mind for some time he wondered what was keeping Aurora. He stared at the restroom door until the waitress stepped to his table. The waitress looked at the untouched food and asked, "Was there a problem with anything?"

Rambo shook his head and replied, "No everything was good." Then as the waitress pulled out the bill and placed it on the table she said "The female has left the restaurant, would you like her plate wrapped up?"

Rambo looked shocked, and surprised, and then he mumbled, "She's gone!" But he snatched up the bill and looked at the price, and pulled out a $50 bill and handed the money and the bill to the waitress and as he started to get out of his seat the waitress asked again, "Would you like a to go bag?"

Rambo shook his head and as he quickly walked away he said, "No change either!" Within about twenty-five long strides he was outside of the restaurant. The white Range Rover Sport was gone. He stood thinking to himself for a moment as he looked around parking lot and the area.

Then he shrugged his shoulders and stepped to his black on black S550. He eased gently behind the steering wheel. He gathered his thoughts, emotions, and stability and then revved up the powerful AMG engine and rolled out.

Chapter 21

Rambo pulled the S550 into the driveway of his daughter's mom house. Before he got out of the Benz Traci was at the passenger side of the whip. He unlocked the doors so she could get inside, and after she was seated she looked at Rambo and noticed his face held a very serious expression.

Traci asked, "What's wrong Bo?"

He just shrugged his shoulders, but his mind traveled with endless amount of thoughts. She understood him…she could tell he had something on his mind. She spoke with a subdued, whisper as she said, "It's Aurora, huh!" Rambo's expression reassemble into a frown: but crumpled and revealed his pain and frustration, but he asked, "What's with this love thing, ma?"

Traci pulled out a blunt and asked, "Do you wanna blaze?" He shook his head, but said, "You can."

After she fired up the blunt and exhaled some of the smoke she said "Well first, I aint a bitch hater…but I was a lot of jealous. I'm keepin' it 100…I was really mad, and in my CooChii just because I could see you and her was feeling some type a way, but don't get me wrong-y'all looked kinda good together".

Then there was a slight tremor in her voice. She said, "But, I think you had your nose way too open for her, especially so soon."

Rambo nodded as he sat with unreadable eyes and a expressionless expression. Then Traci said, "Bo you can't be lovin' these females so quickly… for one, you still have all your daughter's moms, and I bet that I'm not the only one that woud get back with you."

Rambo was unable to subdue his smile, but he said "And here comes the game, huh?"

Traci smiled as angelic smile as her eyes glowed with love. Then Rambo whispered, "Look here Ma, I aint really built for a relationship, I mean…my lifestyle really interferes with me and relationships, but for real my heart beats for a true love. You know how I am…I love easy, natural, and effortless. It's just my natural characterstics."

Traci was high form the blunt now she whispered eagerly, "Yeah I know huh". Then she looked at Rambo and said, "But you're mean…you also hate easy, natural, and effortlessness…that's what happened to us. You started hating me."

Then as she looked at him, her expression crumpled revealing a silent anger. They stared into each other eyes for a short moment. Rambo could sense her attitude was beginning to boil over. Traci could sense that also, but she smacked her tongue and with an envious tone asked, "Where is she at right now?"

Rambo leaned back against the driver side door and replied, "We went out to eat at Red Lobster, but she got upset and left me sitting at the table."

Traci laughed a soft calm laugh and said, "Left you for real! What did you do this time!?!"

Rambo shook his head with a hopeless expression etched across his face as he softly answered, "It was my fault, not Aurora's…I made an effort to love when I really didn't give myself the full permission to go there, na-mean."

Traci nodded her head as excitement jumped into her voice as she said, "Bo you know yo ass cant handle what your heart does…you love too strong and too quick. Your love is way too hard control. Then she asked well I aint trying to be noisy, but how long have you been fucking with her?"

He shrugged his shoulders as he sat with intense concentration. Then after a brief moment he said, "It aint been long at all, but in the short time it was, I opened up to her…I know I shouldn't have done that, but something shook up my thoughts."

Then a flash of anticipation gleamed into his eyes, but Traci's eyes darkened with hate as her expression frowned with annoyance. Rambo gauged her expression and asked "What wrong now, ma?"

Traci shook her head and smacked her tongue as she replied, "Your what's wrong….you letting these females walk right into your space and take control. That's why

Lee-lee was over at your condo flipping a nutty… She knows yo u too. She knows that you let these broads find their way into your heart."

Then Rambo smiled a teasing smile and replied, "See Traci, I let them and y'all find a way into my heart and into my love…but I know the what, when, why, and who about me and my love, and I love-to love simply because of my conversation. I flow naturally about love and relations…I believe everything I let roll off of my tongue…so I fall in love with my own conversation every time I catch myself feeling myself."

Traci smiled a beautiful smile as she listened to him, and then he continued after a brief moment and whispered, "So I guess I really be falling in love with myself…but when things go left I always find myself disappointed for the simple fact that you women don't be comprehending what I say as much as I find myself comprehending myself…you hear me!"

Traci nodded as she listened to him, but in her high from the weed voice she said, "Like now, huh…you're really tryna be feelin' yourself, huh!"

Rambo made a smirk and shrugged his shoulders, but he said, "Kinda you know, but for the most part I'm tryna get my mind outta this rut, na-mean!"

Then they say quiet thinking in their own thoughts, until Traci broke the silence, "So what are you gon do Bo, are you gon go chasin' after that girl?"

He put a finger to his lip to shhh her as he sat unmoved and silent. The inside of the s550 was so quiet they heard his heart beating. Rambo asked, "You hear that?"

Traci leaned up and tried to listen to what he was hearing, but she shook her head and whispered, "Un-un, what am I listening for?"

Rambo's expression twisted into a smile, and then he softly and smoothly said, "It's my heartbeat…it's echoing through the silence. That's what it sounds like when love touches your heart."

Traci smacked her tongue and rolled her neck. She reached for the door handle and opened the door. As she tried to get out of the car Rambo shook his head and said, "Naw ma' don't run, you gotta hear this…you can't be intimidated by love!"

She quickly snatched her attention away from him and yelled, "Nigga-Please! I aint intimidated by shit…it's just that I can't hear your heat beating, so that pretty much means that your heart is not beatin' for me!"

Then she stood out of the Benz and looked back at Rambo, and said, "Bo you know I love you in my own way, and I know you just like you know yourself."

Rambo listened with sincere curiosity, but Traci smiled without any humor as she said, "Go do you…any mutha-fucka that knows better knows that you're about to go find Aurora…and me personally…keepin it 100, I hope you find her and make it work out. Because at least you seemed happy and if you're happy wit' her, then I'm happy for you."

Then Traci pushed the passenger side door close, but Rambo let the window down on the passenger side and as Traci started to walk back to the house, he yelled, "What if I don't find her, can I come back and get at you, remember you said you was feelin' some type'a way?"

She looked back over her shoulder with a mean expression froze on her face, but she yelled, "Fuck you, Bo! Get yo-flash light and go find you some more Colorado Coochii to fall in and outta love wit'!"

Rambo just smiled a little, and then as the window eased back closed he looked at his iPhone and whispered, "I just might go lookin' for her wit a flash light!"

But instead he shook that thought off his mind. He revved up the powerful but quiet AMG engine in the s550 and backed out of the driveway and rode out headed home.

Chapter 22

It was later on in the evening, and Aurora had been riding around in circles. Her mind was unstable…her actions were unpredictable. She had been crying ever since she left the Red Lobster's, and Rambo. Her face, make up, and her normal beautiful expression was smeared and displaced. She was driving with no particular destination, just driving just how her mind was traveling…in circles.

When she realized where she was, her ringtone sounded. She looked at it with a hopeless expression, hoping it might be Rambo, but that expression was quickly replaced with frustration, anger, and hate, because it was Poetry…but she still answered the call, and excitement screamed through the phone as Poetry yelled, "What's up, bitch! Where you at?"

Aurora's expression betrayed a hint of doubt about Poetry, but she replied, "I'm pullin' on your parking lot right now…what's up over there?"

Poetry laughed, and said, "Aw-you know me, just tryna kick back wit a few of my homeboy's."

As Aurora parked the Range Rover, she said, "I'm here, I'll be in after I get myself together, aw-ight." Poetry yelled back, "Okay bitch, that's what's up!"

Aurora sat her iPhone down after the line went dead. Then she sat staring blankly at her twisted looking expression in the rear view mirror. Her mind raced as she tried to make sense of what Rambo had said to her about Poetry, and after a few minutes of analyzing her thoughts Poetry appeared at the passenger side of the Range Rover.

Aurora looked at her with cautious eyes as started gauging Poetry's expression. But Poetry looked her normal self as she asked, "What's up Aurora?"

Aurora shook her head and shrugged her shoulders desperately as tears sprang back into her eyes. Poetry rushed around the Range Rover. She dropped everything she had in her hands and opened the door, and asked again, "What's wrong, Aurora? What is it?"

Aurora slowly eased from the Range and whispered, "Rambo!"

Poetry stood with a brown extension cord over her shoulder, she was unable to control her grimace as she repeated,

"Rambo...what did he say...I mean, what did he do...I told you he was a dog ass nigga!"

Aurora's anger exploded as her expression twisted into an expression of disbelief. She snatched the extension cord from Poetry and wrapped it around Poetry's neck as she yelled, "Bitch how could you! I thought you was my girl!"

Aurora pulled and yanked on the extension cord using all the strength that she could come up with, trying to choke Poetry's life right out of her body! She spoke low as she squeezed the extension cord, "Bitch, you know your shit is all wrong...and way waaayyy too messy! How could you insult me like that?"

Poetry's body started to slowly crumple down to the ground, with her life creeping away from her. Aurora's consciousness of reality kicked back in, she realized that her anger had taken her self-control and temperament. Her consciousness was back alive in her mind.

She realized that Poetry's life was slowly seeping away from her body. So she snatched the extension cord from around Poetry's neck and stood over her body as she struggled to grasp for air and the rest of her life.

Aurora stared at poetry with an unbreakable grasp, her jaws was clench tightly revealing the intensity of her anger as she dangerously threatened, "Bitch, I shoulda choked the life outta yo-shady ass!"

Poetry looked hopelessly up at Aurora and pleaded and cried, "Why Aurora, why are you doin' this to me?"

Aurora raised a delicate eyebrow as she glanced around with surprise, but she said, "Oh bitch are you gon still continue to insult my intelligence…" her anger continued to burn. Pain gripped her expression as she pulled the extension cord back and began to forcefully strike Poetry all over her face and body. Literally whippin' her ass! Poetry screamed, yelled, and cried out in pain as each violent lash struck and tore into her skin.

Aurora hollered back with excitement in her voice as she screamed back threats and promises with each lash and whip of the extension cord. Her rage continued to gain full strength as she inflicted her pain and anger on Poetry…that is until some people from the apartment complex came out and looked on with interest, and as the niggas that was in Poetry's apartment came to her rescue.

Poetry's face and body had been tortured, cut, and bruised from the repeated blows. The niggas pulled Aurora away, but she continued yelling, "Bitch, next time I'ma kill yo-ass!"

Poetry could not do or say anything…she just lay on the ground in pain with her mind in a daze as her homeboy's comforted her and her pain. Aurora stood

unmoved by Poetry's cries, but then one of
the niggas yelled to Aurora, "Bitch get yo-
whip and Tre-up!"

Aurora was close to the edge of losing
her mind…she stood smiling with pleasure,
and as she looked at Poetry one more time
with imaginary obligation and quietly
reassured, "Now bitch the next time I see you
I promise you that I won't let any of the
useless life you have remain in your hoe-ish
body!"

Then she walked away with an
unwavering confidence to her Range Rover.
She dropped the extension cord to the ground
next to Poetry's other things, and climbed
back into her whip. She revved up the
powerful engine, and as she slowly rode away
from the crowd her eyes sparkled with delight
as happiness peaked back into her expression
behind her tears, and as she rode out, she
waved to the police as they looked at her
puffy bruised face from so much crying when

they pulled up on the scene of the brutal and well calculated assault.

Chapter 23

Rambo sat at his desk in his personal office at home. He sat deeply wrapped in his own thoughts. It had been a number of days that passed by, and he remained stubborn by not calling Aurora, or anyone for that matter. After he shook himself back into the moment his eyes landed on the electric calendar on his desk. The day was Friday June 27th, and as he stared at the day and the date he whisper, "I've been in this rut waaay to long...I gotta keep it pushing!"

Then as he raised and stepped away from his desk his iPhone sounded off. He had been ignoring his phone calls all week, but he answered this call, and after he said, "Hello!" He stood in a dazed trance listening to the voice on the line until he replied, "Well if she calls again, tell her that I'm on my way to see her."

He stood next to his desk with a questionable look, as he let his mind wander. He looked around with an expression of disbelief as his voice spoke out, "In jail, for assault! What the hell is up with Aurora?"

But he shrugged his shoulders, and after he questioned his own thoughts for a few minutes, he gathered himself together. Then he quickly showered and was dressed, and was standing looking at himself in the mirror. He felt an energy surge throughout his body.

He asked his reflection in the mirror, "What was that?"

He smiled to himself making his reflection smiled back, and then he whispered, "That was the spirit of love coming back into my heart!"

He smiled another teasing smile at himself, and then he said, "Let me get in traffic so I can check up on my emotions!"

Then he declined the steps, and when he made it into the garage he sat in the Benz, his thoughts continued to race around his mind. He shook his mind clear and revved up the powerful but perfectly smooth engine. He opened the garage door and said to himself again, "Well I gotta see what's up, at least I'll know how I really feel…plus I wanna know why she ran out on me like that!"

****

Rambo parked outside of the Denver City Jail in downtown Denver, but as he walked inside through the doors a rush of anticipation surged throughout his body. He Thought, "This is not a comfortable place," but he continued on through the security check, and on to the visiting booth. Visits were held on a T.V. monitor.

As soon as he sat at the screen he realized just being down there made him nervous, but it was past that now, because the screen lit up, and there was Aurora. As soon as Rambo looked at her his expression frowned. She looked bruised from so much crying…her eyes were puffy and filled with heartbroken tears.

She waited on him to pick up the phone, once the receiver was next to his face; the tears slowly crawled from her eyes. However, she let a smile ease onto her expression as she whispered, "Hi babe!"

His frown continued to crumble with anger, frustration, and empathy as he stared blankly into the screen at Aurora's face. Aurora stopped, smiling and looked with a sulky expression as she asked, "What's wrong babe?" Her voice was missing its edge; she was missing her beautiful mannerisms.

Rambo shook his head and softly let his voice and emotions communicate, he said, "I'ma get you outta here, ma'…I'ma get you out today!"

The tears continued to flow over her smooth skin, but she whispered, "Babe my bond is $100,000…I can't ask you to go through that kinda trouble."

Rambo held his normal composed expression for a moment, but then he asked, "Why did you leave me at Red Lobster's?"

Aurora tried to wipe away her tears, but that was useless, because they continued to flow heavily, but she replied, "Babe, I wish I woulda stayed wit' you…cause when I left it went bad. I went all bad! I lost my mind; my thoughts had me driving around in circles for the longest. I rode around Poetry's neighborhood for the longest, I mean-until I let my unstable ass mind persuade me into goin' over there." Rambo gave her his undivided attention.

She continued, "That bitch called, I pulled up in her parking lot and beat her ass! But I thank God, because as I choked her with that extension cord I seen her life draining from her body…I really wanted to kill her ass. I really felt insulted by her tryna get at you, especially after I told her how I feel about you. But like I said I thank God, cause I know it wasn't anything else that could've stopped me from squeezin' the life outta her ass!"

Then Rambo apologized, "I'm so sorry ma', I know I shouldn't have mentioned that to you…but don't worry I'ma get you outta here."

Aurora shook her head as she looked into the monitor, and as she spoke her voice was serious, "Babe I really can't let you do that…for the reals, I already know that I feel some type'a way about you, and I've been sittin' in here wishing that I didn't walk out on you…let alone I know I won't wanna even be out there without you."

Rambo raised his hand as he calmed her from rambling on and on, but he said, "Ma', ever since you've been gone my balance, my atmosphere, my harmony…I just mean-my everything has been throwed!" His voice held her attention completely like the harmony of a singer.

He continued, "I've been so gone, I haven't done nothin' but write. My condo hasn't been cleaned in about a week. Why? Because your fragrance fills every room, and my heartbeat is on the same vibe as yours. I've been struggling too."

Aurora looked and she saw that the time was running out, about to go blank in a few seconds, she quickly spoke, "I'll clean the condo babe…I love you!"

Then the monitor went blank. Aurora wasn't there anymore. Rambo stared deeply with his emotions and thoughts at the blank screen. He remained seated until the next visitors came to the visiting booth. As he walked away from the screen he whispered softly, "I love you too, ma'!"

As he exited the building and walked to his s550 thoughts crossed his mind about the$100,000 bond. Once he was seated behind the steering wheel. He mentally weighed all his options about bonding Aurora. He was poised but still confident as he asked his self, "Do you really think you're doin' the right thing?"

After a while of wrestling with his thoughts he nodded, and said, "I know love has a lot to do wit' this, and that I can't let my shit be flawed by love alone…but in this case love might be worth more than money."

Rambo eased back out of the Benz and headed back to the City Jail entrance. He stepped into the records office a female asked, "May I help you?"

Rambo pulled out his wallet and pealed out his Visa Card and said, "Yes, I wanna make someone's bond." The female looked up Aurora's name and replied, "This bond is 100,000 thousand dollars."

Rambo nodded his understanding and passed her his Visa Card. The female smiled and whispered, "Must be real special, huh."

Rambo didn't respond as he stood with no emotions in his eyes as he waited until the process was over. When he signed all the necessary paper work, he retrieved his Visa Card and then turned and waited until Aurora would be released.

Chapter 24

Rambo sat calm and poised in front of the Denver City Jail as he waited patiently on Aurora to be released. As he waited he was experiencing some very intense emotional reactions. He sat listening as his heart communicated the feelings that flow within him. He understood that he was being influenced by himself, his own tender feelings. He was being affected by his true emotions. But he felt he was doing the absolute right thing, and that's exactly what his heart told him.

As people passed him he sat undaunted out on the front of the City Jail. The longer he waited the more certain he was about feelin' some type'a way, and about posting that much money for Aurora's bond. He was extremely unrelenting over all. He just nodded to his inner thoughts and smoothly whispered to his self, "What does love have to do wit this!" But after a few moments he whispered again, "Everything! Love has everything to do wit this!"

Then he listened as his thoughts replied, *"This love will be untouchable...it will be everything."*

Then Aurora came walking out of the entrance of the building with a smile etched across her expression, and as soon as she and Rambo laid eyes on each other he lit up like a bright light as he looked at her. She made it to him in three long strides. She wrapped herself completely around him, and the tears instantly began to flow down her face. They stood wrapped embraced in each other's arm for a long moment. Then Rambo finally stepped back and softly asked, "Let me look at you…are you aw-ight?"

She didn't look as if she's been in jail for a week anymore. She still looked really good to him. He actually smiled and said, "Ma' I miss you…I miss seeing you, and you still look good, ma'."

Aurora made a noise with her mouth, "Psst, please! I look like a jail bird!"

Rambo nodded as he continued to look her over from head to toe, but he said, "For real ma', you're in your natural self…you look even more beautiful, more special to me, perfect to me, ma'."

Aurora blushed and then replied, "Thank you babe." Then she wrapped herself back around him and whispered, "Thanks for getting me out babe, but can I ask you a question?"

Rambo stepped away from her briefly, and looked at her with a questionable expression as she thought quickly in her own head then she said, "Babe, can I come stay with you...I really don't have anywhere to go that's gon make me feel the way I feel right now."

Rambo stood blankly for a few seconds, and then she said, "Babe I promise I won't do nuthin' but love you absolutely unconditional...I promise babe, I don't ever wanna be away from you again." She stared into his eyes with an unbreakable grasp and again without a hint of doubt she said, "Babe I love you, and there isn't anything in this world that I know more than that…I really know that I love you, and that's the way that I am feelin!"

The words that flowed from Aurora's mouth, from her sexy sultry voice were precise and direct. It was as if she studied what she was going to say, and how she would say them. Everything she said had sincerity at the base of her harmonious tone. Everything flowed so natural. Rambo sparkled with delight, as he was at a loss for words.

Aurora looked around real quick and asked, "Where did you park at?" But she noticed the Benz before he could respond…then she said, "And you don't have to answer that right now, I can see in your eyes babe that you love me too." Then she pulled his hand and said, "Come on babe, please get me away from down here, I don't care if I do have to live in a shelter."

As they walked up on the Benz Rambo said, "Ma' come here." Aurora walked right up on him, and he wrapped his arms around her and showered her as passionate and intimate as he could with a loving kiss.

Then after their kiss, he said, "Ever since our first night together ma', I've been feelin some type'a way…but now over the past week I know how I'm feelin'…I'm loving you ma'! I mean, loving everything about the way I'm feeling, about the way you make me feel…you make me feel, see taste, touch and hear love. You have all of my senses making sense to me."

Tears rolled down Aurora's face, but she happily glowed inside of her tears as she listened to Rambo pour out his heart. Then he said, "Yes ma', you can come live with me…yes ma', I would love to have you in my life like this, and as long as we can keep up wit' this chemistry that our hearts have."

Aurora smothered his lips with her perfectly curved full lips and mumbled, "For-ever babe! That's nuthin', our chemistry is natural, we gon last for-ever...I love you and you love me, babe...it will be simple for us to love for-ever."

Then they stood wrapped in each-other's arms letting their hearts beat into each-others heart beat until they were on the same rhythm...one rhythm, making themselves into one love! Then Rambo whispered, "Come on ma', I know you're hungry...let's go get us some good eating, and then let's go home so you can really relax and kick back in my kingdom, your new palace."

Aurora smiled, and then as she eased out of his arms she whispered, "Yes babe, that's exactly how I want my next few days to be...kicked back and relaxed!" Then they both eased comfortably into the s550 Mercedes Benz and rode out.

Chapter 25

Rambo pulled the s550 Mercedes Benz on the Benihana Restaurant's parking lot, and as he shut the engine off he looked at Aurora's expression. She looked kinda questionable so he asked, "What's on your mind, ma?"

Aurora looked at him and asked, "Babe, how do you fall in love with someone and not even know their real name?"

Rambo smiled a little, and then replied, "How you know my real name aint Bo!"

Aurora softly and playfully punched him and smiled as she said, "For the reals, babe…I love you and I know that, but I don't even know the person that I'm in love with."

Rambo looked serious as he replied, "Well if you think that's somethin', how do you spend $100,000 on a person that you've only been knowing for really a weekend…how do you explain that as love?"

Aurora sat with a calm expression, but her mind raced as she sat in deep in thought. Then Rambo said, "Darnay Rhythm."

Aurora's face lit up as she resounded, "Darnay Rhythm…that's your name!" Then she smiled with happiness and happily said, "Yes! Now I feel like I'm makin' progress!"

Rambo nodded and said, "Well, now that you know who I am, can we go enjoy some exquisite service."

Aurora continued to let her mind activate until she looked surprised at Rambo and excitedly asked, "You paid the bond in full…a full $100,000?"

He shrugged his shoulders and nodded once and then he whispered, "Yeah ma', now you owe me a full $101,000, and I intend to collect that in full!"

Aurora suspiciously at Rambo for a brief moment until she cracked a smiled, and then sarcastically replied, "Well babe you better put a ring on it, because its gon' take me a lifetime to repay you that kinda money."

As Rambo pushed the driver side door open and started climbing out of the whip he said, "A life time is what I really want...I want love, and I want it to be *UNPHADABLE!*"

Rambo locked and armed the alarm on the Benz as Aurora ran around the Benz and wrapped her arm around his arm as they walked into the entrance of the restaurant.

■■

Rambo never paid any attention to the black Cadillac Escalade that followed him from the downtown area. The Escalade was driven by a female named "Sexy". As she trailed Rambo, she talked on the iPhone to Poetry. Sexy laughed as she parked the Escalade on the Benihana parking lot. But she spoke as she watched Rambo and Aurora walking to the entrance of the restaurant, but she said, "I can't believe you let that bourgeois ass bitch get at you like that!"

Poetry replied in a serious voice, her emotions, angers, jealousy, and envy's could be heard as she said, "I told you that the bitch snuck me…she didn't give it to me fair!"

Sexy made a smirk and the sound, "Psst, Bitch what the fuck ever! Then what was her reason for getting at you?"

As Poetry yelled, her anger screamed through the speaker, "The bitch didn't get at me…and all this shit is behind that nigga! Yeah, cause of Rambo…he tried to get at me, but I didn't give that nigga no play, none whatsoever!"

Sexy subconsciously mumbled, "Yeah bitch what the fuck ever, you aint gotta lie to kick it…you probably tried to put that moist pussy on that niggas lap, but got your sensitive ass pride wounded when he dissed yo-ass!"

Then as Sexy watch them enter the restaurant she said, "It looks like she just got out of jail…didn't you say her bond was 100 racks or somethin?"

Poetry mumbled in the phone, "He must'a got her ass out…I told you that nigga is sittin' on some major bread, and if we play this shit the right we can put our hand all the way in his game…and get papered up, and I can get my revenge!"

Sexy nodded as she sat back soaking up her own thoughts, and then after a few moments she asked, "So what do you want me to do?"

Poetry exhaled a deep breath and replied, "Don't trip right now, and now that I know the bitch is out I can start to apply pressure…just over here big sis so that I can let you know how it's about to go down!"

Sexy clicked off the iPhone and sat staring at the entrance of the restaurant for a few moments. Her thoughts raced around her about everything that Poetry has said thus far, but she whispered to herself, "If this nigga has this kinda bread, I'ma just have'ta invest some real game in his ass." Then she nodded as she slowly rode past the black s550.

****

Rambo and Aurora stood intently and curiously looking out of the restaurants front door watching the black Escalade as it slowly rode off the parking lot. As Aurora peered through the window she softly whispered, "That's Poetry's older sista…they call her "Sexy"."

Then Aurora's voices kicked into another tone as she said, "But I really don't see why they even call her Sexy, especially with her lookin' like some lady dude!"

Rambo laughed as he continued to let his eyes glance over the rest of the parking lot, but he softly replied, "Now they actin' like they wanna really play this shit raw, huh!"

Then he turned and looked Aurora in the eyes and calmed her with a friendly expression as he nodded once and said, "Since Poetry wants to get dirty in the game, I'ma get some people to the same game that she wants to play."

Aurora's confidence wavered as she looked with a hopeless grin. She wrapped herself around Rambo and replied, "Babe I don't want no-one to get hurt...I really didn't mean for this to blow up like this, I was just mad that she tried to interfere with my emotions...my love!"

Rambo shrugged his shoulders and whispered, "Ma' you didn't do anything wrong...in a sense, all you did was fight for what is yours...and whatever else goes on now, you just let me handle it...because I already told her ass not to ever come to my condo…and if she havin'people follow me, then she's still violating my space. But oh well, let me deal wit that, you just keep your mind clear and continue feelin' me."

Aurora looked and listened with skeptical eyes as she thought to herself, *"He doesn't seem worried at all!"*

Then Rambo said, "Let's gon and get us some good food in our bodies so that we can function properly and think correctly." Then they stepped. Aurora followed Rambo as he lead the way into the restaurant's dining room area to a private table.

Chapter 26

As Rambo and Aurora drove from the restaurant Aurora looked around being paranoid. Rambo looked over Aurora and recognized how shook she appeared so he said, "calm down ma', you don't have worry about Poetry. If she or anyone else tries to mess wit' this love we gon' just have to handle our business, na-mean." Aurora nodded but continued to look around nervous with cautious eyes.

Then as soon as Rambo pulled the s550 up to his condo anger leaped onto his face. Trouble flashed into his eyes as he looked at the open front door of his condo. Aurora glanced to what he was looking at. She gasped a deep breath when she noticed the door wide open. When she turned back and looked at Rambo all she could see was his profile, but she saw the intensity of his anger as he pulled a heat from the floor under his feet.

Aurora whispered, "What's wrong, babe?"

As she watched him making sure that his heat was ready for whatever it was called upon to do, but he softly but seriously replied, "I don't know ma', but you stay right here while I go check on my crib."

He stepped from the Benz with a black towel draped over his left hand concealing the big .45 magnum. He looked quickly over and about the area, but everything seemed normal, but he stepped with an alert and lively pace. In less than 7 strides he was at the front door.

He aimed the covered .45 magnum and quietly, but quickly eased into and throughout the condo. Within a minute flat he was back at the front door. He nodded for Aurora to come inside. When Aurora walked through the door tears slowly crept out of her eyes.

Rambo stared at her as she entered the door, but she whimpered and whispered, "I'm so sorry, babe...I really am, I didn't mean for any of this to happen. I don't know why Poetry could be doin' any of this."

Rambo looked away from Aurora, and his focused landed on his security system. It was still active an armed. The green light flashed its readiness. He shook his head, and in a low tone said, "No ma', this was not

Poetry…this was someone with a very high intellect about alarm systems."

Then he pointed to the systems key pad on the wall and said, "You see that ma', that shit is actually armed right now…whoever got in here deactivated the alarm system."

Then Rambo held up a news paper clip that was about a 15 million dollar diamond heist in Paris. Aurora's mind raced and shook like a California quake as she looked at the news paper clip questionably. Her mind became filled with an endless amount of thoughts about the news paper clip.

As Rambo stared attentive at the clip about the diamonds he asked his self, "What the fuck does this have to wit, and why was it left here?"

Aurora stood in a trance looking lost in her own thoughts. Rambo's jaws clenched tightly revealing the intensity of his anger as he looked around with surprised eyes. Then his eyes landed on a mason jar that was full of what looked like diamonds. He stared hopelessly lost at jar, and whispered, "close that door, ma'."

After Aurora closed the front door Rambo remained sitting at the dining room table staring seriously at the diamonds. Aurora stood quietly behind him as he softly asked, "Do you think these things are real?"

Aurora shook her head and softly answered, "Un-un, I think they're fake as a $3 bill, because I think no-one would that many real diamonds lying around anywhere."

Rambo smiled a little but it was without humor. Then when he opened the jar it had a note attached to the inside of the lid. The note read, "These zirconia's may be over your head, but the real meaning of them are right at the tip of your nose, and diamonds are a girl's best friend."

After Rambo read the message he sat letting the words of the note circle around in his thoughts for a few moments, and as he wrestled with his thoughts Aurora stood behind him. Her eyes were full of uncertainty and fear. She seemed very uptight and nervous, but when Rambo looked back over his shoulder at her she tried to maintain a poised, calm, and confident expression by looking hopeful.

But after Rambo whispered, "Diamonds are a girl's best friend," he asked, "Do these things have anything to do with you?"

Aurora's confidence, calmness, and poised posture were crushed. Her expression turned to innocent surprise. She looked at Rambo with anxious and wide eyes. Shock took a grasp of her; she didn't know how to respond. She stood froze with intense concentration. Then Rambo's lips twisted into a smile as he replied, "Calm down ma', I'm just tryna add a little humor to the moment...I know this can't possibly have anything to do with you."

Aurora smiled lightly and a sigh of relief eased onto her expression. Then the doorbell sounded, and it shocked them both catching them off guard. Rambo's hand instantly reached for the heat as he stood onto his feet. Aurora followed behind him as he walked to answer the door. Rambo yelled, "Who is it!"

The voice on the other side of the door said, "It's me Bo, it's "Wacc"!" It was his neighbor from the next condo over. Rambo opened the door after he tucked his heat away in his waistline. He held a composed expression, but he said, "Aye Wacc, what's up bruh?!?"

Wacc looked calm with a friendly expression, but he said, "My nigg, I just came by to make sure you was good, cause I seen some very intriguing gentlemen over here inside your condo...I thought nuthin' of it, but when I seen you pull up in your whip I realized that you were not there when they

247

entered…I just thought you know, especially if you don't already know, na-mean."

Then Wacc asked, "Do you set your alarm?"

Rambo shook his head and said, "Yeah, but it wasn't set today."

Wacc nodded, and replied, "Well is everything good…them guys looked like some very serious gents."

Rambo nodded and said, "Yeah I'm good, and thanks for keepin an eye on things." Wacc nodded, and then turned and walked away.

Next Rambo closed the door and locked it. Then he turned and faced Aurora. Fear and panic was etched on her expression as she whispered, "I'm scared babe!"

Rambo nodded, and then as he sat down on a stool in the kitchen, but he mumbled, "My entire peace feels like it has been violated… My entire foundation is shook."

Aurora eased back over next to him. She confronted him as she wrapped herself around him in an embrace. She felt a reaction of fear. Her body began to quiver as she held him. She whined, "Babe, let's leave Denver for a while…lets go on a vacation."

Rambo shook his head and said, "Naw ma, I can't afford that right now, na mean…I just spent a 100 racks getting' you outta jail."

She squeezed him tighter and continued, "Babe money aint a thing…I can pay for everything…but I wanna leave right now, right this moment!"

Rambo looked up into Auroras' face tryna gauge her expression. She looked very serious as she nodded, and said, "Babe, I have some money…I actually have a lot of money…but it won't do me any good at this moment. Its only valuable if we leave and leave right now."

Rambo continued to stare at her with a questionable look until he asked, "What's a lot of money and what is a vacation to you?"

Aurora raised an eyebrow and shrugged her shoulders as she replied, "Enough money to go anywhere in the world that you ever wanted to go and we can go there right now."

Rambo thought to himself for a brief moment, and then he said, "I wanna go to Jamaica…or I wanna go to Barbados."

Aurora pulled him off the kitchen stool and smiled excitingly as she said, "Come on babe lets go there, let's go right now."

Rambo stood looking at her with a surprised expression. He let his curiosity wonder just what may have accelerated her motivation. Aurora could see that he was given his thoughts a lot of attention, so she continued to speak holding a grasp of his attention. She didn't want to give him time to think.

She began to pull him towards the front door as she said with sudden excitement, "Babe we have to leave right now and I mean right this minute…just believe me!"

Aurora knew what was going on. She knew the reality of the diamonds was catching up to her. Then her expression turned ugly and dangerous as she spoke with a subdued whisper, "It's not safe here…this condo is no longer a peaceful palace, we really have to leave."

Rambo's questionable expression grew and stretched across his face as he watch her nodding with a panic expression as she pulled him out of the door. When they made it to the Benz, Aurora nodded her encouragement as she demanded, "Let me drive babe!"

After he tossed her the keys she eased gracefully around to the driver's side of the Benz. They both sat comfortably in the whip. Aurora revved up the powerful but quiet and smooth engine. He looked at her with sincere curiosity, and then with a serious tone he asked, "Does this have anything to do with the newspaper clip that's about those missing diamonds, and about my condo being broken into?"

Aurora peeled off, and as she peeled away from the condo she glanced at Rambo with alarmed eyes and said, "Yes babe, everything! This has everything to do with the diamonds,' but instead she focused on the traffic ahead of her as she continued to speak, 'I'll explain everything to you, but not until I know that we are safely away from here. Now what's the quickest way to D.I.A.? (Denver International Airport)

Rambo pointed and directed her into the direction of the airport, and as he reclined in the passenger he said, "I wanna know every motherfucking thing! Because having to leave on such short notice-this shit has got to be serious."

Aurora nodded as she drove, but she replied, "Yes, this is real serious…this is life or death serious, and like I said, once we get in a comfortable place, I mean-once we reposition ourselves-I'ma tell you everything about Paris, the diamonds, I mean-everything dealing with me."

Rambo stared at her profiles and for some reason he was strangely impressed, and for a long while as she drove, he let his mind question what and who she really could be, and what she was really all about. He listened to his inner self saying, "*I knew it was somethin' about this breezy, now I gotta find out about everything, and especially that bread she talking about havin'!*"

Aurora sped over the speed limit on I-225 racing and rushing to make their speedy getaway heading to DIA, and leaving the problems behind, including the problem of Poetry.

TO BE CONTINUED…

But stay in tune…Because there is a lot more about Aurora, in part 2 "Still Feelin Some Type'a Way…also be on the lookout for "Long as My Bitches Love Me". "Issues" and many more novels by Success.

Thank you for reading my imagination, and I hope you enjoyed yourself as much as I enjoyed myself when I was writing this.

SUCCESS

Any respond Email at success.bo314@gmail.com or at The Aurora Series on facebook.

Printed in Great Britain
by Amazon

31498719R00145